Dear Clementina

Dear Clementina

Letters from one Border Terrier pup to another

COLIN BURKE

ILLUSTRATED BY W.H. MATHER

Matador
9 Priory Business Park,
Wistow Road, Kibworth Beauchamp,
Leicestershire. LE8 0RX
Tel: 0116 279 2299
Email: books@troubador.co.uk
Web: www.troubador.co.uk/matador
Twitter: @matadorbooks

ISBN 978 1784624 231

British Library Cataloguing in Publication Data.
A catalogue record for this book is available from the British Library.

Printed and bound in Malta by Gutenberg Press Ltd
Typeset by Troubador Publishing Ltd, Leicester, UK

Matador is an imprint of Troubador Publishing Ltd

I'd like to acknowledge the following contributions made to the creation of this book… namely

Jan and Hughie Jones, who provided the initial stimulus to write it
John and Gill Atty, who provided the encouragement to continue with it
My wife Monica, who provided patience and the editorial supervision to develop it
My sister-in-law Sylvie who provided the technical supervision to produce it
And to Stanley, who provided sufficient raw material to fill it.

Colin Burke

And talking about dedications,

I'd like to dedicate this book to my mum and dad, Spider and Molly, to Debbie and Mick up there in County Durham, who gave me a proper start in life, and to all my mates in Manchester and Cartmel.

Yours forever,
Stanley

11th May

Dear Miss Jones (may I call you Clementina?),

Firstly may I say how nice it was to meet you in the park yesterday. Sorry I was a bit shy and reluctant to stray too far from Colin's legs, but believe it or not, you're the first dog outside of my immediate family that I've met up with. With not having seen any of them for ages, I was starting to wonder if I'd ever enjoy canine company again, and you being a twelve-week-old Border Terrier pup the same as me made our meeting especially good.

As I told you yesterday, what with my sleeping in a cage and only exercising in the back garden with its high walls and fences, I'd started to believe that I was in a prison down here in Manchester, albeit an open one, serving time for some unknown crime I'd committed. Well, maybe not exactly *unknown* to be fair; I suspected it may have had something to do with Colin's socks.

You see, when I moved in with Colin and Monica a few weeks ago, one of the first occasions when the Old Man praised me was when I turned up in the living room with a dusty old sock in my mouth. "Good grief," exclaimed Colin, "where's he found that? What a good dog you are, Stanley!" It seems he'd lost that particular sock, with its distinctive blue toe and heel, months ago and, hey, I'd found it and he had the pair again. "Never mind about Border Terrier, proper Bloodhound you are, lad," he said, obviously chuffed.

In truth, it hadn't been hard to sniff out the old sock that had been gathering dust just under their bed. I'd had a bit of a struggle to claw it out, but once I'd got it in my mouth I triumphantly carried it downstairs like a shot pheasant. I didn't think it was such a big deal, though, but I quickly noticed Colin's enthusiasm about the whole matter ("Saved me £2.50 finding that sock, the dog has," I heard him tell Monica as he patted and stroked me) and I determined to repeat my obvious success whenever opportunity knocked, as it did, fortuitously, an hour or so later. I was back out on patrol and checking their bedroom when I spotted a couple of his socks nestling quietly on a stool. Without a second thought, I grabbed one in my mouth and, with my tail frantically wagging like a flag in a gale, ran down to Colin in anticipation of the praise that was

surely to come. Well, you can imagine my surprise when, instead of the expected, "Good boy Stanley," I got a stern, "Stanley, drop that!" as Colin ran towards me, arms outstretched and grabbing at the cotton sock.

Now I remembered at that point that I'd played this game a few times before, whereby I'd be chewing a ball and Colin would come over to me and say, in rather a silly voice, "Give me that ball, Stanley, give me that ball…" Then I'd play along with him by running out into the garden and he'd laugh and chuckle as he chased after me to try and get the ball, and we'd have five minutes of fun, frolicking around on the lawn. So I naturally translated, "Give me that sock," in similar vein, and so out into the garden I bounced, and out into the garden he duly followed, shouting and waving his arms as he went. Well, by the time the game was over and he'd managed to retrieve his sock, it was, I've got to admit, rather the worse for the experience and would more accurately be described as an 'ex-sock' to be honest. Apparently socks that cannot accommodate toes because they have large holes where said toes should be fail to fulfil any real purpose, and a single sock on its own is about as much use as a cat in a fox hunt. So Colin was now going to have to shell out £2.50 to replace them and, indeed, by the time a fortnight was up the bill was more like £17.50. But in my defence I have to say that he's proved to be a very slow learner when it comes to securing his assets, and I won't even begin to tell you about the number of his slippers I've disembowelled.

Anyway, with my record of offences against assorted items of footwear, you can imagine my delight yesterday when I was apparently let out on parole and, as if by fate, we met up.

It looks like I've served my time (although I'm still in my cage at night) and can look forward to many a romp with you and that other dog (was his name Barkley?) down there in Fog Lane Park.

Looking forward to it.

Sincerely yours,

Stanley Burke

Heaton Road
Withington

29th May

Dear Clementina,

It was really nice to see you in the park yesterday. Gosh, there were lots of new faces, to say the least, and I was so busy checking everyone's tail-hinges that I didn't get the chance to finish my story about when the dog trainer came to see us.

I'd only been with Colin and Monica for a week or so and with them being inexperienced in most things canine, they were keen to ensure that they were bringing me up properly. Apparently, when he was a lad, Colin's family had a dog called Paddy, but he'd come from a dogs' home, fully grown and conditioned, so Colin had no real clues from that relationship to help him deal with a new puppy. Interestingly, one day I heard Colin musing about Paddy, whom he described as a 'mongrel', a breed that I've not heard mentioned in the park but one that appears to have been very popular in those days. Colin reckons he was half-Border Collie, half-Alsatian, half-Cocker Spaniel, half-Whippet, with just a dash of Labrador. Seemingly, 'taking Paddy for a walk' each morning consisted of opening the back yard gate and saying, "Good dog, Paddy, see you tonight." The dog was then free to run off up the cobbled alley to re-enlist with one of the many gangs of dogs that roamed the parks and streets in those days, messing about and playing all day, until late afternoon when he'd tell his mates that he'd see them tomorrow and went home for his tea, barking outside the back door to let the family know he was back. That was, of course, unless he and the rest of the pack had camped outside the residence of a bitch on heat, where they'd hang around for ages, like paparazzi on the trail of some indiscreet celebrity, in which case the 'call of the wild' would mean it would be supper time at the earliest before Paddy got home. Cor, how times change, hey?

Anyway, after a bit of research on the internet, a trainer was sent for and Alex duly turned up for Project Train Stanley. Now by this time I'd become a bit shy and nervy when the door bell rang and had a tendency to hide under the coffee table when people called around. When I'd first arrived in Withington I was quite the opposite and had been very keen on new faces and smells, happily jumping up to make friends with each and every new visitor who came to see Monica's 'latest addition'. All this changed, however, when one particular guest made me more than a little wary of strangers.

She was a rather large lady and, after a long hard ring of the front door bell, she'd bounced into the lounge like a baby rhino and swept me up in her arms saying, "Who's a little darling, then?" In her enthusiasm she then lifted me high above her head, shaking me gently and looking into my startled eyes, exclaiming, "Who's a lovely puppy? Who's a lovely puppy?" as I looked down at her from just below the ceiling. Now I don't know about you, Clementina, but when I get excited or frightened I tend to 'leak', as Colin politely terms it, and leak I most certainly did on this occasion, all down the lady's bare arms. And to be honest, she's very lucky that I didn't end up doing something more substantial, because I'm not afraid to admit it, I was petrified – I know now that I'm definitely afraid of both heights and, not surprisingly, of big ladies. Anyway, since that short but not-at-all-sweet trip into the stratosphere, whilst I still enjoyed leaping up at Colin and Monica at every opportunity, whenever the front door bell rang I'd rush to hide under the coffee table in case it heralded the arrival of another over-zealous guest who wanted to reintroduce me to the dizzy heights of the ceiling.

And so that morning that's just where I was, under the table, when Alex entered the lounge. He wasn't the instructor initially engaged for the job and was actually standing in for a colleague who was ill. Unable to spot any dog in the room, he assumed that his new trainee was locked up somewhere and he was frantically going through his colleague's notes to check what was required. "Is this the Doberman that's been chewing the kitchen furniture?" he enquired without looking up from his file, "or the Pit Bull that attacks postmen and bit the policeman who came round to investigate? Or is it the Alsatian that won't stop running round in circles, barking and chewing its own tail?"

"Er, it's none of those," replied Monica, almost apologetically. "It's the ten-week-old Border Terrier who likes to jump up."

Alex looked bemused, but Colin quickly added, with a certain gravitas, "And he steals socks!" It was at that point that I stuck my snout out from under the table and Alex looked down at me and saw the size of his task.

"We'll start from scratch then," he declared, only for Colin to chip in, "Oh, no need for that, my friend – his mother taught him how to scratch," at which point Alex raised one eyebrow and half-smiled, politely.

Anyway, the gist of the first session was that we Borders don't need much training, but just a bit of guidance in certain specific areas. As for me leaping up, Alex explained that it was natural for a puppy to do this as one of its first instincts was to greet its returning mother by jumping up towards her mouth to try and get any regurgitated food that she may have on offer (I could see Colin grimace at the very idea), and to deter me they merely needed to mimic a disapproving mum and growl at me! Well seriously, Clementina, you'd have laughed as the two of them took up the challenge and set about perfecting their growls, which sounded more like something between grunting and groaning to be honest. But once they'd eventually mastered it, we all went out into the garden for the next phase of the lesson. We then had a fun half-hour out the back, with me jumping up and Alex growling, then me jumping up at Monica and her growling, and then it was Colin's turn, and then they were all growling, and I was jumping up and down, and barking along with them to keep the fun going. But, like all good things, the whole exercise came to an end and it did so when the lady next door called out in a rather nervous voice from the other side of the garden wall, "Is everybody OK over there? Do you need any help?" Well, with that we all rushed inside, with me still barking and them sniggering and giggling like naughty children.

As for measuring the success of the whole lesson, I was actually getting a bit fed up of leaping up at every opportunity and had already decided to reserve my jumps for special occasions, such as when the pair of them return home after leaving me on my own. And I stopped hiding under the table after hearing Monica warning visitors that if they lifted me up high, on their own heads be it – in every sense! Not surprisingly, everyone seems to have got the message.

Anyway, see you soon.

Yours as ever,

Stanley

Heaton Road
Withington

10th June

Dear Clementina,

Crikey, what a load of fuss about a couple of squashed croissants! This weekend, a simple show of affection on my part somehow turned into a mini-crisis which you'd think only direct intervention by United Nations peacekeepers could resolve.

The nub of the problem was that, whilst I normally exhibit a maturity well beyond my six-and-a-bit months, as you know I do have that rather puppyish habit of jumping up when Colin and Monica enter the house. With an enthusiasm and a style that would bring credit to a young trout, I invariably leap up in a show of affection which the wife of a returning sailor would surely be proud of.

Anyway, on this latest occasion Colin had just popped down to Didsbury in preparation for his much-treasured Saturday morning routine of sitting on the patio with a large cappuccino, freshly baked croissants and the *Guardian* sports section. As he returned through the front door with his purchases, the paper under his arm and with his keys in one hand, croissants in the other, he was, to say the least, ill prepared to cope with the running leap of canine affection that was about to be visited upon him. I'd actually been out in the garden when I first heard his key in the lock, so I'd got up a really good lick of speed by the time I arrived in the hall and bounded toward him, with all my four feet off the ground. Now I have a firm opinion about the garden, Clementina – if you don't want me to have mud all over my feet, don't encourage me to spend time out there where there's loads of it. And nobody should be surprised if a small leaping dog, especially one with muddied feet, has some material effect on a newspaper that tumbles from under its carrier's arm down onto a floor where the by now falling puppy, in accordance with all the laws of physics, is bound to land with both significant kinetic force and momentum. And when the said carrier of the Saturday *Guardian* then lets fall a pair of freshly made croissants which are contained in the flimsiest of flimsy plastic bags, it should come as a shock to nobody that the gyrations of an excited dog rip the outer pages of the newspaper and then squash the products of the local

patisserie into a shape more akin to that of a couple of Auntie Bessie's Yorkshire Puddings than an archetypical French confection.

Colin, to put it mildly, was not amused. Using words that I had not heard before, and do not particularly want to hear again, he bemoaned the blatant destruction of his Saturday morning schedule. Monica, obviously suppressing laughter, was much more sanguine and pointed out both that the paper was still just about readable, and that the croissants would taste the same whatever their shape. "Tell that to sixty million Frenchmen," retorted her husband, adding, "What do they look like?" *A dog's breakfast* was my immediate thought, but I considered it best to keep my own counsel on this occasion.

To be honest, I suspect my jumping problem stems from my 'Home Alone' syndrome that I've developed. I do not, repeat *not*, enjoy being left on my own in the house whilst Colin and Monica go out enjoying themselves for a few hours. I can always tell when they're about to pop down to the Red Lion or wherever, not just because they start changing their shoes and putting their coats on, but because they always give me a pig's ear to chew whilst they're gone. Have they never heard of Pavlov's dogs? For those salivating canines a bell ringing meant that food was on its way, and for me a pig's ear means that my pair are off out on a jaunt without me.

Now I have to confess that I do not always behave well when I'm left alone and flying solo around the house. Usually they've closed all watertight doors and tidied things away, but I have been known to find a lone newspaper which needs some serious shredding, and on one occasion a casually positioned box of tissues meant that they returned to see that snow appeared to have fallen early in Withington this year. Anyway, after what always appears an age on my Tod Sloan, when

I hear the taxi pull up outside and the front garden gate opening, hours of pent-up frustration, affection and anticipation all come together to produce repeated leaps and licks and nips.

On such occasions I think their guilt at leaving me alone for hours means that they put up with such flamboyant and uncontrolled behaviour, but they're certainly not impressed when I act likewise when Colin has merely popped out to the shops for five minutes. Something must be done, they've decided, so it's back to the training manual, I'm afraid. Water sprayed up my snozzle appears to be on the cards – not looking forward to it one bit, but I suspect it'll work. I'll let you know how I get on.

See you when this rainy spell clears.

Yours as ever,

Stanley

22nd June

Dear Clementina,

Sorry I haven't been around for a week or so, but, golly, what a strange time I've been having – and talk about 'be careful what you wish for!'

Now as you know, since I arrived in Withington I've had to sleep in a cage (it's called a 'dog crate' to be accurate, but it's got metal bars and bolts and I get locked up in it every night, so you tell me). Anyway, whilst I feel surprisingly at home sleeping in there, my ambition has always been to spend the night in a nice comfy basket in the kitchen. So for some time I've been hoping that, once I'd proved that I was able to hold-my-own in the house hygienically, so to speak, I'd be trusted to make the move into a basket, and then eventually, oh dream of dreams, maybe upstairs onto the matrimonial bed, snuggled up next to Monica. Now I do know that Colin's always been opposed to me making the big move upstairs, for reasons of both principle and space, but one morning a week or so ago I thought that things were progressing and he was at last consigning the cage to the scrap heap. It all began when I came across him taking my white furry blanket and blue spotted cushion out of it, together with my favourite toy, Dolly. He then proceeded to dismantle the whole contraption, noisily folding down its metal sides before trundling out of the front door with it under his arm.

I was still musing on the potential pleasures of a future sleeping in front of the Aga, and wondering when the basket would be installed, when I was put on my lead and all three of us piled into the car and set off on a drive. After we'd been going for about ten minutes, with me sat on Monica's lap and happily looking out of the window as we went along, we drew up outside a house which I immediately recognised. It was the place where I knew a really nice old black Labrador called Tyler lived, along with an equally nice young lady called Hayley and her family. We'd spent an hour or so there a few weeks ago and the great thing I remembered about Tyler was that, not only was she a wise old thing, but she also let me play with her as much as I wanted. And, even when she got tired after a while and had to lie down, as older dogs tend to do, she was still happy to let me jump all over her and nip her ears and bite her collar and what have you. So it was with real joy and anticipation that I pulled at my lead as I bounded from the car and into her house, leaping up at her to renew our acquaintance, and the pair of us were immediately sniffing and nipping and rolling, and generally having a grand old time.

After twenty minutes or so of frolicking about, even I was getting a bit tired and, guessing that it would soon be time to go, I thought I'd best go and find Colin and Monica to see what they were up to. So I checked around the living room, and then in the back room, but there was no sign of them, and then I ran sharpish up the stairs and checked out each of the bedrooms, but all to no avail.

Well, by now I was getting a little worried, but I worked out that the only place left where they could be was the kitchen. But, as I strode in there, imagine my shock when it wasn't my folks that I found but – wham! – it was my cage, there in Tyler's kitchen, all assembled and upright, complete with my white furry blanket and blue-spotted cushion neatly in place, and with my beloved Dolly all snuggled up inside. And what's more, there was neither sight nor sound nor smell of Monica and the Old Man. Well I can tell you, Clementina, I was now completely confused by it all, and not a little upset to say the least. So I ran straight back to Tyler, who was outstretched in front of the fire, and I blurted out my concern. What was happening to me? I asked. Was I nothing more than an itinerant puppy, with nowhere permanent to call my home? Having spent my first nine weeks with my mum up in County Durham, I'd been in Withington with new people for a couple of months or so, and now here I was, over in Bredbury, with yet another lot, nice though they may be. Was this my fate, to be a 'have-crate-will-travel' dog, doomed to forever wander from place to place, having no sooner settled down in one house than I was whisked off to another?

By this point, Tyler could see I was near to panic, so she got me to lie down next to her and breath slowly and calm down so that she could help me understand what was going on. Once I was settled and snuggled, she quietly told me not to worry, assuring me that Colin and Monica would be back in a week or so, and that they had merely gone on their 'holidays', not left for good. I was still rather confused, but she proceeded to explain that, every now and then, people like to get away from home for a week or two, to see different places, eat different things and smell old friends. And when they can't take their dogs with them, they arrange for their beloved pets to go on holiday themselves, and that's exactly what I was doing over here in Bredbury – I was on holiday, staying in a guesthouse for dogs (and a very good one at that, she was keen to point out). Her final piece of advice was that I should just sit back, relax and enjoy the experience.

And that's precisely what I did, Clementina. Once I'd got my head around the idea of a change being as good as a rest, I settled down for a whole week of fun, with lots of walks and lots of playing with Tyler, and lots of hugs and strokes from Hayley. So if you're ever in the same position, my friend, follow my lead and do just what Tyler suggested – put on that hangdog expression that's second nature to us puppies, and play the poor abandoned orphan. It's working a treat for me, with Hayley and her kin giving me plenty of treats and smothering me with sympathetic cuddles all week, whilst they declare, "Poor Stanley, have you been left behind? Don't worry, we'll look after you – they'll be back soon."

And as I lie here on the sofa, after a long frolic with Tyler and with Hayley gently stroking my tummy as she consoles me again, I'm thinking, *Don't hurry back folks – ever thought of a long cruise?*

Anyway, I trust that back they will surely come, and very nice it'll be to see them; but rest assured Clementina, there are worse ways to spend a week than having bed and board in Bredbury.

See you when I get back.

Yours, as ever,

Stanley

Heaton Road
Withington

30th June

Dear Clementina,

When last I wrote I was in Bredbury, telling you how laid back I was, literally at times, lodging with Hayley and Tyler, so I didn't think I'd be particularly excited when my folks returned to pick me up. How wrong was I!

As I've told you before, whenever either of them comes through the front door I'm always ready, tail wagging furiously, back end waddling excitedly, and I then smother them with affection by way of licks and jumps and nips. But even I have to admit that my greeting this time, after an absence of what seemed like ages, could be considered a touch over the top. Monica went so far as to describe it as an example of my 'berserker dog' impersonation, which I do when I run round and round in ever increasing circles, then out into the garden and around the greenhouse, then back into the lounge and several times around the sofa, before collapsing, panting heavily, onto my back to have my tummy rubbed. On this occasion, as soon as they came through the door I was up and down like a kid on a pogo stick and, unsurprisingly, I was leaking as I went. After a minute or so Colin noticed that I'd accidentally leaked on his nice new holiday shoes, but, as ever, Monica was on the side of the righteous (i.e. me). "Well, you should have changed before we came to pick him up," Monica told him rather unsympathetically as she looked down at the speckled and spotted deck shoes. "Anyway, they'll dry out OK," she added, but I don't think she was totally convinced.

After a few minutes it happily all calmed down and Hayley duly reported on how I'd behaved during my stay and, for the most part, she gave me straight As. However, she did mention that she'd given me a C minus in one specific aspect, and a rather embarrassing one it was too. Now I'll hold my paws up and be the first to admit that, on occasions during the week, I'd been a touch over-zealous in my affections with Tyler, but that said, I feel that 'humping her on a regular basis' as Hayley described it to Colin, was an unnecessary exaggeration. I know that in the past you and me and Barkley and Poppy have discussed the 'humping habit' a number of times, and I appreciate that you girls are at a loss to see the point of it all, whilst I find the whole exercise rather therapeutic, and I'm sure it's completely innocuous.

However, it was the Old Man's reaction to Hayley that really intrigued me – he immediately lost his voice! His lips were moving and he was obviously mouthing words, but nothing seemed to come out. No matter how much I strained to hear him, I couldn't catch a word – me, who can hear a fox scratch his ear half a mile away! Hayley, on the other hand, seemed to be able to read his lips, and nodded in acknowledgement as he silently spoke to her. I tell you what, Clementina, that's some trick.

Anyway, as I sat there rather baffled and looking up at them, from one to the other, the only clue Colin gave was when he held out two fingers and made like a pair of scissors, and then he let slip out loud that something had been 'arranged for next week'. I've no idea what it all means – maybe he's getting his hair cut.

On a completely different matter, I meant to ask you the last time we met if you've ever come across digestive biscuits? The reason for asking is that they're a very popular confection around here apparently and, for some reason, we Borders, when nice and clean and fresh, are reputed to smell just like them. Last week Monica tantalised me by letting me actually sniff one, but though she wouldn't let me eat it, I did manage to get a couple of a decent licks and a slobber over it before she anxiously whisked it away and put it out of my reach on top of the fridge, saying something about dogs being wheat intolerant, whatever that is. You'd have laughed, though, when a minute later Colin came into the kitchen and, peckish as always, picked up the biscuit and finished it off in a couple of chomps before Monica could say a word. He's obviously not intolerant of wheat… or of puppy spittle, come to that. Anyway, what's odd is that I now keep getting a whiff of the same biscuit smell in the park, especially when the wind's blowing from over the football pitches; really pleasant it is. Apparently there's a place called McVities a mile or so away in that direction and that's where the smell comes from. I can only suppose that there's a Border Terrier puppy farm over there; more research needed, I suspect.

One thing that I find strange, though, is that everyone is so careful that I don't get so much as, say, a scintilla of wheat germ down my gullet, and yet they take me to a park where there's always all kinds of really tasty rubbish scattered around for a puppy to eat. Mind you, even I have to admit that scavenging around does have a tendency to play havoc with my innards at times. Take last week, for example; I was out with Colin in Fog Lane and I'd managed to race off and devour two old tissues, a couple of sandwich wrappers and something which even I struggled to identify before he came running up and put me back on the lead, declaring sternly, "Stanley, when will you learn that there's no such thing as a free lunch?" *Well you could have fooled me*, thought I, having just filled my boots at no charge to anybody whatsoever. But I have to concede that I did see his point the next morning when we had to go the vets (yet again) to deal with my resultant 'trash-induced digestive problem', as he called it. He ended up having to pay £35 for the privilege of having me put right and he was obviously not at all amused, remaining virtually silent in the car all the way back home – except, that is, for the occasional 'free lunch, my backside' that he grumpily muttered, to no one in particular. Still, I'm sure I'm worth it.

See you soon.

Yours as ever,

Stanley

Cavendish Street
Cartmel

17th July

Dear Clementina,

(Bow) Wow, what a week! I told you on Sunday how good it was to be back home after my time in Bredbury with Tyler and her family, and how I was looking forward to a bit of peace and quiet back in Withington. Some hope that was!

On Monday before breakfast we were out walking through the village, seemingly with no specific destination in mind, when *Hey, I know the smell of this place!* thinks I. There were lots of smells of lots of dogs, pesky cats and even those half-daft rabbits, and yep, you guessed it – we were at the vets. Now every time I've been there before, whilst the treats and the strokes have been in abundance, so too have the jabs and pills and sprays up the nose, so I had no great expectations that my morning was going to be a particularly fun one. But actually, all that happened was that the lovely girls there gave me lots of cuddles and hugs, put me in a nice comfy crate, shaved a patch of hair on my leg, gave me a little jab and then left me alone. And after that I had what can only be described as a truly first class sleep – you know the type, really deep, with not a sign of running rats or rabbits to chase. And I was definitely reluctant to get up from such a wonderful slumber when they woke me what must have been hours later so that I could drive back home with my folks.

I'll tell you what, though – when we arrived back in the house, Colin began acting very strangely. I can't imagine why but he seemed to keep on apologising to me, saying things like, "I'm sorry Stanley, but it had to be done.' What exactly 'it' was I hadn't the slightest idea, and he didn't elaborate. Then a bit later he lifted me up carefully, placed me on his lap and, as he gently stroked me, started going on about me 'never missing what you've never had', and how it (that 'it' again) 'would all turn out for the best'.

Well, I was still quite sleepy as he was droning on and didn't pay that much attention, but as I started to doze off, I heard his wife telling him not to be so stupid and reminding him that they'd had 'it' done to a few of their cats years ago without, as she put it, 'all this guilt thing'.

16

"Yes," he said, "but you're not a man – you wouldn't understand. And anyway, with the cats it was because the vet said it'd stop them smelling and going out at night." At that, Monica gave him a wistful look, and I'm sure I heard her mutter something under her breath about how, if that was the case, there's many a man who'd benefit from the same. But at that point the tiredness finally overwhelmed me and I fell into a deep sleep before I could hear if he had any response.

To be honest, I felt a bit off that night (I hardly touched my dinner), and somehow I ended up with a big blue inflatable collar around my neck. It's a bit of a bind that collar, to tell the truth, especially when I want to lick a ticklish scar that's suddenly appeared 'down there'. I remember when they were putting it on I had a quick peek and something is definitely different in the undercarriage department. I can't quite put my nose on it, but the contours aren't quite the same as before and it all looks a bit flatter. I seem to recall there being a couple of little lumps nestling there, but they appear to have gone missing – maybe they're like my puppy teeth and, because I'm getting older, they've dropped out somewhere. I must remember to have a good search round to see if I can trace them when I'm next free to snuffle around the house; maybe they've fallen off in the garden – I'll check out there too. But that's for another day. With regards to the collar, at least I'm not wearing it all the time and when I am, people find it rather fetching. I'm actually getting lots of, "Ah, what a cute little sweetie" and, "Poor little Stanley" when I'm out and about with it round my neck, so I'm not too bothered really. Mind you, when it's not on, Monica watches me like a hawk and if I make the slightest move of my head in the 'down there' direction she's on me in a flash, pushing my snout in the opposite direction and diverting me with one of my toys, especially one of the squeaky ones.

Anyhow, we're up in Cartmel now, so I won't be able to see you in the park for our usual roll-about with Barkley and Poppy. I heard Colin mention something about me needing 'rest and recuperation' so they've got me on the long lead for our walks through the woods, and so all ideas of messing around with other dogs up here are strictly out. I think it's something to do with that scar I mentioned (I've heard them talking about it to other people) and I suspect that, as it keeps getting less and less itchy, I'll be off the lead and at it with the rest of the gang before you can say 'Jack Russell'. Anyway, I'm definitely getting back to my old self, eating my dinner as usual and looking forward to a couple of days at the weekend when those big horses charge around the park up here, chasing each other.

By the way, can you let Barkley know I'm OK? The other week he did warn me, as one dog to another, something about vets, scars and collars but I wasn't sure at the time what he was talking about. "Male matters," he said, but I thought he meant something to do with chasing postmen or the like – how wrong can you be!

Anyway, have fun without me, and see you next week. I'll let you know when I get back.

Yours, as ever,

Stanley

Cavendish Street
Cartmel

19th July

Dear Clementina,

For sale – one inflatable blue collar, hardly used!

Yes, great news: the collar is off and I'm free to 'access all areas' to my heart's content. In truth, I only had it on for the first two nights when Monica let me sleep on her bed (the Old Man was consigned to a spare room in case his tossing and turning woke me up), and then a couple of times when we ventured into the streets of Cartmel. Colin was telling people that my scar was getting less licks than your average mini Magnum (whatever that is), so today we had a ceremonial deflation of the collar of constraint wherein he put it down on the carpet, took out the stopper and cautiously sat on it (interesting noise, that was). Anyway, I don't really know what all the fuss has been about; I'm back to my old chipper self and life is sweet.

You'd have laughed this morning when, early on, I discovered that the side gate on my crate was open. As you know the crate had been with me when I was over with Tyler and Hayley, and when Colin put it back together up here he must have missed securing the side entrance. I hadn't noticed it on previous mornings, but when I stretched as I woke up first thing today it just popped open. So

out I trotted, and up the stairs I strode, and onto the bed I jumped – and boy, did they look surprised! (What is it about people? You give them lots of licks one time and they love it, but do the same as they lie fast asleep in the early morning and they act like startled pigeons.) Anyway, the outcome was that I was scooted out into the garden pronto and had peeped and pooped before the Priory clock had pealed seven. Colin has now locked the offending gate and so it's back to normal tomorrow.

Monica subsequently had a bit of a go at Colin for his rather cack-handed DIY skills. In his defence he said that they didn't do metalwork at his school, they did Latin instead.

"Some use that is," she said.

"Well," he replied, "at least I know the Latin for 'The damned dog's escaped'." She was not amused.

So an early start for the household and it's off to the Cartmel Races we go this afternoon. I don't know if you've ever been horse-racing but I came for the first time in May, and it's all a bit strange, if I'm honest. A gang of horses put men on their backs and chase each other around a field, jumping over hedges as they go. That part I understand and I'm sure that for those involved it's great fun. (I did try to join in at one point, but a big grey mare gave me a look which said, "Back off, kid!" in no uncertain terms, so I didn't need telling twice.) As for my lot, all that seems to happen is that before each race Colin goes over to a man and gives him some money; then he watches the race and when it's over he shouts, "Bugger!" Then he goes back to the man and does the same thing all over again. In May it was seven races and seven 'Buggers' and then home for tea at six. Not sure what they get out of it but it'll be the same again this afternoon, no doubt.

Well that's it for now. Back in the park Wednesday or Thursday so I'll see you then and we can catch up on all the news. Give Barkley and Poppy a nip for me.

Yours, as ever,

Stanley

Cavendish Street
Cartmel

29th July

Dear Clementina,

I know we'll be meeting up in the park before the week is out but I just wanted to share with you a couple of things that I learned at the weekend. The first is, and hold onto your bone here, there are lots more of us Borders than we thought! If you remember, we reckoned that, what with all our brothers and sisters and our uncles and aunts and whoever, and with Murphy and Bella and the other Borders we've seen in the park, there must be about thirty or forty of God's chosen breed in the world – not so! Last Sunday my folks took me to a country fair up here in the Lakes and there were loads of us, of all ages and several colours. I counted at least fifty and, after talking with a few of them, they reckon there are even more who weren't there. So by my reckoning it looks like there could be a couple of hundred of us spread across the country – there's a thing to ponder.

Anyway, when we first arrived at the fair, it being a really hot day, lots of us dogs gathered along the shore of what they call Lake Coniston. There were scores of us, paddling and splashing and jumping around in the water and really lapping it up, in every sense of the word. And as I wandered about, checking everyone's tail-hinge as I went, I came across an old Border standing quietly up to his dew claws in the cooling waters. Now there was definitely something unusual about him which I couldn't quite work out, but he soon let me in on his secret when we got into conversation and he told me that he was blind – Clementina, he couldn't see!

Now, just before I met up with Blind Bobby, as he's known, I'd been chatting to an old hand about the dog shows that were going on in the fair, divided as they were between hounds and terriers. It turns out that the farmers up here have these two kinds of hunting dogs, side-by-side; the hounds are bred to chase, like the cavalry, after foxes and rabbits and hares until they run to earth, and the terriers ("The poor bloody infantry," as my informant described us) are reared to charge down the escape holes after the prey to risk life, limb and snout either killing them or chasing them back out so that they can be seen off. So, assuming that he'd lost his sight in an encounter out hunting, I asked Blind Bobby what it was that had done it to him – a wounded fox or a cornered rat, or maybe even a mad rabbit?

"Chicken," he replied immediately.

"What?" exclaimed I, completely confused. "A chicken scratched your eyes out?"

"No lad," says he, "… I ate too many of them!" And that's why, Clementina, I felt I had to write straight away to warn you and the rest of the gang, and anyone else we meet: if we eat too much we'll all go blind!

It turns out Bobby had a real appetite for chicken (as well as for beef and offal and, well, just about anything you've ever heard of, really). His people loved him so much that they fed him as and when he looked hungry and, I don't know about you, but according to Colin, I always look hungry. Eventually, some things called 'dire beaties' got into him and Fat Bobby, as he was by then being called, became Blind Bobby, and as well as not being able to see, he gets a needle stuck into him every day; how doubly awful is that? And it's not simply a matter of eating and eating until one eye goes and then you can stop and go on a diet – they both go at the same time!

I've got to admit, Clementina, it knocked the stuffing out of me to hear his story and it certainly put me off my tea that night (although by breakfast the next day I was, fortunately, back to my old self).

So, we must spread the word to all the dogs throughout the parks of South Manchester and the woods of Cartmel – we must NOT, repeat NOT, eat too much!

As for me, you'll be pleased to know that I'm back to rolling around with other dogs now, my scar having virtually disappeared. I heard Colin commenting that, despite my operation, I was still prone to 'adopting the brace position' with other dogs, but Monica says I'll get over it, whatever that means – remind me to ask Barkley or Billy about it when next we meet. And remind me to tell you about Colin's identity crisis.

But that's all for now. It's ever so hot up here and Monica has taken to wrapping me in wet towels… Heaven.

Yours as ever, and see you soon,

Stanley

Cavendish Street
Cartmel

30th July

Dear Clementina,

Well, as you'll have noticed we're not in Manchester at the moment, having rushed up to Cartmel to take advantage of the fine weather.

We had an interesting walk today to a place nearby called Humphrey Head where, legend has it, the last wolf in England was seen off.

As soon as we arrived there and got out of the car I was buckled onto the long leash and we passed through a stretch of land that was full of animals that I'd not come across before. Colin duly advised that they were sheep and cows and warned, with that serious voice he occasionally adopts, that if I ever chased after such creatures a Blinkin'farmer would shoot me. Blinkin'farmers are, according to him, responsible for most of the unpleasant things in the countryside, be it blocked footpaths, slow-moving traffic, dead badgers or, more worryingly, people's dogs getting shot. They own all the land and all the animals such as the sheep and cows, and Colin repeated his caution that if I ever worried a Blinkin'farmer's livestock I'd end up very quickly as a sad Townie's deadstock. So remember Clementina, up here when you're walking through fields with animals in them, it's, "Clunk-click, every trip!"

As for the poor old last wolf, he was chased-down by a pack of bloodhounds (so much for canine solidarity!) and put to the sword, I assume by a Blinkin'farmer, hundreds of years ago. I had a good sniff around the very spot where he's reputed to have finally expired, and ceremonially cocked a leg, by way of silent tribute.

On a different matter, did I mention that Colin was a tad depressed the other day after the Coniston Country Fair? It transpires that he'd seen all those other Borders there, of all ages and a few sizes, and it dawned on him that I wasn't really a young puppy any more. Now you'd think that me getting older would be no one else's concern except mine, but that's not the case. You see, strange as it may sound, it turns out that men of Colin's age are invisible to all younger females and, equally strangely, this invisibility apparently diminishes when such men go out with a puppy. Seemingly, puppies turn all females into quivering jellies, stimulating their innate maternal instincts, and men out

walking said puppies get to bask in their reflected affection. As you can imagine, this does their ageing egos no end of good, but, sadly for them, as we young dogs get older, the affect on females starts to wear off and the men's invisibility returns, until the only females who can still see them are their nearest-and-dearest, other dog-walkers and parking wardens. So, as I am now losing my puppyish good looks, Colin is having to resort to pronouncing loudly to passing females, "Oh yes, he's still a puppy you know – he's only six months old." This tends to have the desired effect, but how long he can get away with it is anyone's guess. I suspect he'll be lying about my age for some time to come yet – it's quite sad, really.

Anyway, I'm off to play tug with him in the garden, but before I go, a word of advice about thistles, a plant that I came across on Humphrey Head. Now you obviously won't ever make the mistake that I did of cocking a leg up against one, but be warned, don't even sniff them – neither experience is pleasant and neither will ever be repeated by yours truly, I can tell you. I'll pass on the advice in more detail to Barkley and Billy when I see them at the weekend.

Yours as ever,

Stanley

Heaton Road
Withington

2nd August

Dear Clementina,

Sorry we missed you in the park today, but due to the uncertainty as to when the rain would arrive, we were out well before breakfast. (In fact, I don't actually eat anything in the morning now, ever since I had that dodgy tummy and the vet recommended that I just have one meal a day, and that's in the evening; so first thing in the morning all I have is what's apparently known as a 'fox's breakfast', namely a pee and a good look round!)

Had we met up, I was going to share something interesting I learned yesterday. You are, of course, aware of humans' fascination with 'the bag that dare not speak its name', as Colin refers to it. Virtually everyone with dogs in Fog Lane can be seen at some stage with a neatly tied and often brightly coloured plastic bag in their hand, much to the amazement of those people unfortunate enough not to be blessed with canine company. Interestingly, when I was very small, I heard Colin explaining to a pal how he'd made the transition from 'disgusted of Tunbridge Wells' to 'needs must when your pooch does a poop in the park'. His theory is that puppy owners are paranoid about toilet training their young charges, dreading, as they do, finding a load on the lino or a mess on the mat. So when they're first called upon to 'brandish the bag' in the park, they do so with an apparent feeling of euphoria, accompanied by a strong desire to shout out to the heavens, "Praise be to goodness; it's not on the carpet!" And thus it's with a strangely happy heart that they carry out their onerous task and, after a couple of repetitions, the conditioning is well and truly reinforced and their responses are as hard-wired as one of Pavlov's dogs'. (In all honesty, though, the Old Man doesn't do much 'lifting and shifting' as this falls mainly to Monica, but he does go above and beyond the call of duty when required.)

Anyway, whilst I've sussed out how humans deal with that which we find surplus to requirements, I wasn't sure how they managed what was 'not wanted on voyage' of their own. I certainly hadn't witnessed any examples of them in action in the park, nor in the house or garden come to that. But yesterday we went out in the car and, because it was only a short trip, I was allowed to sit on Monica's knee and look out of the window. So you can imagine my surprise when, going through Fallowfield, we passed a big building called Supermarket and saw that there were lots of people coming out of it carrying, yes, you guessed it, brightly coloured plastic bags – and some of them were carrying more than one! My suspicions were duly confirmed when I noticed a big sign on the door saying *Strictly No Dogs Allowed* – and that's understandable, I suppose. Apparently, whilst we canines don't care who sees us as we leave our messages in the park, humans are not so open and certainly wouldn't want us watching on as they did the necessary.

I'm not sure where they deposit their own bags though, but certainly not in the bins in the park where ours end up, so life still holds some mysteries. My best guess is that they bury them somewhere, but I'm not certain.

Anyway, that's it for now. Big week coming up – we're going up to the Lakes for the Cartmel Show and I'm going to meet up with my mum, Molly, along with my sister Elsie and brother Archie. They're what are called 'show dogs' and they'll be strutting their stuff in the ring up there. As you can imagine, I'm really looking forward to it and I'm sure we'll all get on really well.

By the way, did I share with you that Mum was a single parent? Had to bring up seven of us on her own, she did. Not sure what happened to Dad. She never mentioned him; had his way and went away, no doubt.

I'll let you know how it goes. Lots of tears and sniffs, I suspect.

Yours, as ever,

Stanley

Cavendish Street
Cartmel

11th August

Dear Clementina,

Well, talk about things not turning out as you expect them! You'll recall that I was getting very excited about meeting up with my mum and family at the Cartmel Show and, as you can imagine, the feeling of anticipation increased when the day duly arrived and we wandered through the showground on our early morning walk. There was already a real buzz about the place (especially near the beehive exhibition) as prize sheep and rams were herded into their corrals by white-coated shepherds with lively dogs, posh horses were getting put through their paces by even posher riders clad in red jackets and black boots, and good-looking cows and bulls were having their coats groomed with big brushes and fancy hair-driers wielded by handsome young farmers in tweed caps. You know, it was as if someone had scripted and designed the whole event as a build-up to the great reunion of me (the long lost puppy) and my beloved mamma, Molly. Contrary to expectations, however, it turned out that she hadn't got round to reading the script!

It all started promisingly enough when we turned up at the dog show around noon and almost immediately spotted Mum's party of six dogs on the far side of the parade ring, all sitting quietly and sharing three crates. As you can imagine, I was seriously choking at my leash once I'd spotted Molly and virtually dragged Monica around the perimeter to get to her. And then there I was, at long last, in front of her… my beloved mother. Well, I caught her eye, and she caught mine, and I caught her scent, and she caught mine, and then I caught the sharp end of her tongue as she barked at me to, "Clear off, you little varmint!" Can you credit it? After all the anticipation and all the excitement, and me having even prepared a little speech, and after all Monica's hard work grooming my coat to make me look my best, when that longed-for magic moment finally arrived, the pair of us hit it off like a pair of fighting cocks!

Now Debbie and Mick, who'd brought her to the show, were not at all surprised by Molly's reaction, saying it was par for the course when a mother meets up with one of her offspring. Monica, on the other hand, was as taken aback by it all as I was. But Colin, as is his wont, was quick to analyse what was happening. It was, he declared in that rather highbrow voice he sometimes adopts, all a

matter of evolutionary instincts whereby a bitch was programmed not to 'get involved' with her offspring lest any resulting progeny be flawed genetically, thus putting the survival of the bloodline in jeopardy. Monica, on the other hand, had other ideas and declared that he was talking tosh. With her usual female intuition, she reckoned that Mum reacted like she did because the last time we were together I was repeatedly exercising my growing teeth on her inflamed and overused teat and so, at this, our reunion, she was letting me know in no uncertain terms that she was having no more of that behaviour, thank you very much!

Well, who knows why she reacted as she did, but I certainly backed off sharpish. After an embarrassing few minutes, everything settled down a bit and I had a chat and sniff with my sister Elsie and half-brother Sid, but they were both rather standoffish if I'm honest. So, after a couple more minutes, we moved away with barely a backward glance, and that, as they say, was that. It looks like you and Barkley and the rest of the gang are my family now, Clementina.

There was one thing that I learned from my brief encounter with the family, however, which I was most surprised at, and it's all to do with my name. Now when I first moved in with Colin and Monica I think they took some time to agree on what to call me. In those early days, it quickly became apparent that they couldn't decide between calling me Getdownstanley, Goodboystanley or even Baddogstanley. Eventually they settled on simply 'Stanley', but it transpires that my proper name is, in fact, Raleniro Smash It Up, and I am the duly accredited son of one Cobstone Way River Magic and his dam, Seymour's Bubble and Squeak for Raleniro (that's Molly to you and I). Yep, Clementina, that's right – I was born with a silver bone in my mouth; I'm a duly accredited, one hundred percent pedigree member of the canine aristocracy.

Now it may be that you too are high-born, but if you're not, and before you feel that you need to tug a forelock or bend the knee when next we meet, let me assure you that I intend to renounce my title. Colin is a bit of an old leftie at heart and isn't particularly comfortable with my high-blown status. He's decided that I should 'do an Anthony Wedgwood Benn', and that means that I renounce my title, in the style of a high-born chap who gave up his posh name to become a lowly commoner. So whilst the Old Man did concede that me being named after a punk band record gave me some working-class credibility, that's it – from here on in, it's just Stanley that I am, and just plain Stanley that I shall remain. And anyway, as he commented to his pals in the pub as he recounted the tale, "What's in a name? … as Shakespeare so perceptively observed in *Romeo and Tracy*."

Talking about names, Colin was telling Monica his theory about why Barkley likes to bark so much. She reckons it's because he's a Tibetan Terrier and they were bred to guard sheep and bark at rustlers, but Old Smarty-pants thinks otherwise. His theory is that our pal thinks his name is actually Lee, as befits a native of the Orient. So when John or Gill calls out, "Barkley," he thinks it's an instruction and begins hollering accordingly. Gosh, he does come out with some nonsense at times!

Anyway, back down in Manchester soon so see you in the park. Oh, and by the way, Mum came second in the show – won a rosette and lost a son, all on the same day, she did. Ah well, such is life.

Yours as ever,

Stanley

Cavendish Street
Cartmel

15th August

Dear Clementina,

I hate to be the bearer of bad news, but young Albert died last week, during the heat wave. You remember Albert, the French Bulldog who lived in Didsbury and regularly walked through Fog Lane Park? Well tragically he got much too hot when he was out with a dog walker in Cheadle, collapsed whilst running to fetch his ball, and that was that – dead and gone at just fourteen months old.

Monica was obviously upset at the news, as, to a lesser extent, was Colin. In truth, the Old Man had been intrigued about Albert's breed in the past, quoting a chap in the park who'd declared that if he had a dog with a face like that, he'd shave its bum and walk it backwards, but Colin genuinely felt sorry for the poor young thing, and even sorrier for the distraught family left behind.

The day after hearing the news, I heard them discussing Albert's loss and the demise of dogs in general, with Monica referring to a poem on the internet about what happens to us dogs when we die. The gist of it is that we all head off to a place called the Rainbow Bridge which is just this side of Heaven and it's where we all wait around until our owners eventually join us as they too pass away. It's a great place, apparently, where the dear departed spend their days running about with lots and lots of other dogs, through woods and across meadows and beaches, playing with balls and sticks and the like, and generally having a fine old time, just waiting until their folks turn up. Colin, macho man that he is, was having none of it, took one look at the verse and wrote it off as 'doggerel' (which I think means rubbish, but seemed a very appropriate description of a dog poem to me). Anyway, Monica called his bluff and got him to read it out loud.

Well, there he was, reciting it rather sniffily until he got to the point in the tale where one little dog, who'd been there for a few years, suddenly stops running around with his pals and jerks to a halt, standing stock-still – then his ears prick up and he raises his snout to the wind, sniffs and… yes, this is it… he's caught a familiar scent in the air and looks over the meadow to sees his beloved owner running with arms outstretched and hurrying towards him. By now overwhelmed with joy, the dog races over and leaps up into his dearest friend's arms, licking and loving as if there's no tomorrow. But at that point in the poem Colin, tough guy though he thinks he is, started whimpering like a kid with a smacked bottom! I was amazed, to say the least. He couldn't even get to the point where the dog and his owner then happily skip over the Rainbow Bridge to be together forever in Heaven. Unable to speak, he picked me up and was hugging and cuddling me, and crying into my fur – quite embarrassing it was, to tell the truth. Anyway, once he'd pulled himself together he swore Monica to keep the whole episode secret, so mum's the word, Clementina; don't mention it to a soul – there's a hard man's reputation at stake here.

True to say, Colin is not usually a softy and whenever he goes on the internet he often comes across more enlightening information (or so he thinks). He told Monica the other day that his researching had revealed the answer as to why we dogs sniff each other's tail-hinges whenever we meet. All ears, she sat there whilst he recounted the tale of a time long passed when all the dogs in the world assembled for a meeting, and they came from near and far, and some they came by chariot, and some they came by car. And when they were assembled, according to the Book, they each took off their backsides and hung them on a hook (Monica had, by this point, realised that this was not a serious academic treatise). Anyway, whilst all the dogs were sitting down in the hall, some dirty rotten scoundrel shouted, "Fire!" at which everybody fled to the exits. In the ensuing panic they all grabbed the nearest backside off its hook without stopping to check if it was actually theirs, and all ran out and scattered into the night wearing the wrong ones. And this is why, he declared, that whenever dogs meet up with other dogs, they'll even let go of a bone to sniff each other's backside, to see if it's their own.

By now not particularly amused, Monica suggested that he should act his age, and that in future he'd better employed researching the olfactory capacity and socialising habits of canines rather than stupid rugby songs!

Yours as ever,

Stanley

RIP Albert – have fun playing by the Bridge.

Heaton Road
Withington

22nd August

Dear Clementina,

Heaton Road seems to stumble from one drama to the next these days, although the latest crisis could be considered rather more serious than 'the case of the crushed croissants' that caused such a fuss the other month. It all started this morning when Colin let out a loud cry from inside the bathroom where he was taking his daily plunge. Interestingly, when I first arrived down here a couple of months ago, Colin always kept a close eye on me and would let me lie down on the bathmat whilst he wallowed in the bath. But all that stopped when on one occasion, in my playful and loving way, I jumped up at him as he was climbing out. Now whilst the ensuing kerfuffle, accompanied by his anguished cries, didn't merit a trip to A&E on his part, requiring no more than a careful ministration of some TLC and TCP by Monica, it did result in me having to visit the vet, yet again – this time to get my claws trimmed!

Anyway, this morning I was sitting out on the landing as he made his plaintive call and so I was on hand to follow Monica as she rushed through the door to see the Old Man lying in the bathtub holding his leg up and exclaiming, "Look at that, it's a tick! Look at that, it's a tick!"

Well, with barely a second glance, his wife immediately started off down the stairs shouting, "Alcohol, Alcohol!" Now I must admit that I was initially very impressed with what I thought was her seemingly detailed knowledge of dealing with ticks, and so I was somewhat taken aback when, in response to Colin's question, "Is that what you smother the little blighters in?" she curtly replied, "No – I need a large gin and tonic; it's all too horrible. I'm shuddering just thinking about it," as she plainly was.

It turned out that the offending creature was attached to his left leg, just below the calf and he'd initially mistaken it for a large spot. He'd only realised what it was when he gave it a gentle rub, at which juncture he'd issued his startled summons to his wife to come and take a look.

Now as Monica descended the stairs in search of solace from a bottle, I was determined not to leave the pack leader on his own in his time of need, so I swiftly administered soothing licks to each and any part of his body that I could reach, which was quite an area once I'd stood on my back legs and leaned against the side of the bath. By this time Colin was, surprisingly, as calm as you like and he climbed gingerly out of the tub. (I considered that a consoling jump-up at this juncture would be particularly inappropriate so I merely wagged my tail and started to lick his feet dry.) He then called out to Monica to fetch him his iPad, a gadget upon which humans seem to have recently developed a dependency previously reserved for lucky charms. *Wow, this'll be good*, I thought, as Monica handed it to him, *he's going to whack it with his tablet thing*. I was, of course, quite wrong and he wisely used brain rather than brawn and Googled up, *What to do in the event of a tick attack*. Shortly thereafter, the offending creature had been carefully removed and dispatched down the sink to join its Maker, with only a blurred photo on the iPad and a reddish blotch on Colin's leg to prove that it had ever existed.

As for my role in the whole affair, I was quite rightly exonerated of all blame (which makes a change these days), me being as clean as a whistle when it comes to harbouring unwanted guests. In fact, despite Colin's assertion that, "We never had a tick in the house before we got that dog," a detailed post-incident analysis eventually laid the blame fairly and squarely on the potentially fatal combination of short trousers and long grass. Yours truly was actually honourably mentioned in despatches for exhibiting loyalty above and beyond, although Monica's recourse to drink at a time of crisis was duly noted and recorded on her file for future reference.

But you know, we really do have to be careful in this area, Clementina, especially recalling that Barkley was telling us how, with that long, luxurious hair that he keeps going on about, he became the object of a of tick's unwanted affections a couple of months ago. As if such a visitation wasn't bad enough, he'd been scooted around to the vets to get it properly removed, only for that particular medicine man to misdiagnose the parasite as an inflammation of the mammary gland and recommend a dose of expensive antibiotics. Later that same day a second opinion was rightly sought, and saw both the tick and the reputation of the first vet disappear down the drain.

By the way, I hear Barkley is in need of an X-ray on his poorly shoulder; no more rolling about for him. You and I and Poppy can keep doing it, though, and I'll see you soon to have a go.

Yours as ever,

Stanley

Cavendish Street
Cartmel

29th August

Dear Clementina,

I can't remember if I ever told you about Colin's 'First Law' fixation? My initial introduction to it was after I'd been living in Withington for about a fortnight and I was being left alone in the house for the first time. Monica, mother hen that she is, was constantly expressing her concern at the prospect of leaving me on my own, but Colin had been quite insistent that, 'for the benefit of all parties' it was something that I'd just have to get used to. Monica eventually conceded the point, although I noted that as one of the so-called 'all parties' I wasn't being consulted and certainly couldn't see what possible benefit I was supposed to derive from such situations. Anyway, after I'd been with them for a couple of weeks, they duly planned to resume their regular Friday night routine of a trip into West Didsbury for a swift pint down at The Metropolitan followed by a takeaway curry from The Great Kathmandu.

So that Friday around 6.30pm out they duly popped, but just before they left Colin put into operation his puppy containment plan, which had, unsurprisingly, been several weeks in the preparation. Reluctant as they were to lock me in my crate, they'd resolved to give me the run of the kitchen whilst they were out enjoying themselves. The fact that the kitchen had no door to separate it from the rest of the house was overcome by the erection of a B&Q three-foot-high retractable barrier consisting of stiff fabric in a plastic frame. And so, just as they were about to leave, Colin meticulously secured the contraption, confidently declaring, "He'd have to be a show pony to jump over that."

Or a Border Terrier pup to get under it, thought I as he spoke, having already spotted a fatal flaw in the Old Man's construction skills. They hadn't been gone two minutes before, with an agility that came from generations of breeding, I'd shimmied my way under the ill-fitted base rail and proudly made my way out into the hall, and hey, now I had the run of the house.

With all the downstairs doors shut, I found myself standing at the bottom of the staircase peering cautiously upwards. As I pondered my next move, I recalled being upstairs previously so it was with an air of confidence common in most puppies that I clambered up the first flight – I deliberately say 'clambered' rather than 'climbed' because the latter would suggest a degree of expertise that I was yet

34

to master. Anyway, once I eventually reached the top I found to my chagrin that all the doors on the landing were also shut and I now had a decision to make – do I go back downstairs or climb another flight to the attic room which I could clearly see was open and accessible? In truth, it was a decision that was effectively made for me when I realised that, whilst I was getting quite adept at climbing stairs, I was at a complete loss when it came to getting down them, remembering perhaps belatedly that on every other occasion when I'd descended from the first floor I'd been secured in Monica's arms! So up I went.

An hour or so later, I was still gazing longingly down the stairs from my attic viewpoint when I heard the front door open and the rovers returned. I could hear them clearly as they entered the kitchen, happily chatting away, and then I caught Monica's startled cry as she realised that I'd flown the nest! Well, Clementina, I never knew what 'blind panic' was before that moment, but I certainly do now.

"Where's my puppy, where's my puppy?" she half-screamed, as Colin started to race around the kitchen, checking first in my crate, and then under the table, and then in the cupboards, and even in the drawers of the French dresser where they keep the knives and forks! And like a man possessed, he kept calling out repeatedly, "Come on Stanley, lad, where are you fella? Where are you?" – but answer came there none.

Now you may wonder why I didn't bark or whine to let them know where I was at this juncture, but I have to confess that I was rather worried that their shouts and screams meant they were really mad at me, and, having once heard that discretion is the better part of valour, I decided to keep discreetly schtum on this occasion. And even when I then heard Colin embark on a frantic and noisy torch-lit search of the garden, where he kept calling out my name in increasing desperation, and then heard poor Monica rush around to next door to check I hadn't ended up there, I kept my silence. It was only when the Old Man managed to calm down somewhat that he announced, in the manner of Sherlock Holmes that, "When you rule out the impossible, which is that Stanley has left the building, whatever remains, however improbable, must be the truth."

"You mean he could be up the chimney?" enquired a now tearful Monica.

"No, that room's locked – he must be in the attic." And with that, he strode swiftly up the flights of stairs to find me there, innocently staring down at him from my lofty perch.

Well, you can well imagine the hugs and the kisses and the tears of joy that followed – suffice it to say the takeaway was virtually cold by the time emotions had finally calmed down. In fact it was whilst the curry was in the oven being reheated that Colin, large glass of red wine in hand, addressed me from his armchair with a certain gravitas that he seems to reserve for just such occasions. "Stanley,"

he declared, "you really must get to know the First Law of Stairs, my lad – and that is that you must learn how to climb down them at the same time as you learn to climb up 'em."

Anyway, the reason I mention this is that yesterday up here in Cartmel I was treated to another lecture about First Laws, this time relating to streams and rivers. It's all to do with making sure you know how to get out of one before you jump into it, and learning about it was no laughing matter, I can tell you. But it'll have to keep until the next time; I've got to rush now as we're off to the beach again where, interestingly, I quickly learned another First Law, this time about the sea – and it's not about getting in and out of it safely; it's, "Don't drink the water – it tastes horrible!" Happy days.

Yours as ever, and see you next week,

Stanley

Cavendish Street
Cartmel

3rd September

Dear Clementina,

Well, as expected we're still up here in Cartmel, taking advantage of the fine weather, as Colin repeatedly tells his workmates – more like taking advantage of the four pubs within a stone's throw of the cottage, I reckon, but I can't say that I'm unhappy with the arrangement. In fact he's been taking me on regular visits to the said hostelries, whilst telling Monica that such excursions are all part of my 'training'. I must admit, though, that I'm somewhat at a loss to understand just what precise contribution to my education results from me sitting under a table in The Cavendish Arms or The Royal Oak, chewing on a carelessly discarded beer mat, whilst he sups a few pints with his pals and prattles on about the state of the world in general, and the uselessness of politicians in particular.

Anyway, I think I mentioned in my last letter that I'd ventured into a stream up here whilst out on a walk, and it was all bit scary really. Due to the races being on again and our usual route resultantly being out of bounds, we've been walking through a new set of woods which run alongside one of the streams flowing out of the village. They really are great woods, full of smells and traces of foxes, badgers, squirrels and the like, although strangely neither Colin nor Monica seem to pick up on any scents, and show absolutely no interest whatsoever in joining me in rolling in any fox poop lying about the place, no matter how interesting it may be.

With there being lots of tree trunks and timber lying on the ground in these woods, they like to play a game where they stand about fifty yards apart, each hiding behind a tree, and take it in turns to call me to them. My resulting sprints and leaps over the obstacle course of logs and branches have both of them laughing loudly in no time, so I'm keen to keep doing it to ensure they stay fit and active. (The way I see it, I'm not sure that their merely standing around in Fog Lane Park just chatting to the other folks keeps their cardiovascular rate up – they're only exercising, or rather over-exercising, their jaws as far as I can make out.)

Anyway, yesterday morning ten minutes of these shuttle runs had given me quite a thirst (a genuine one, I would point out – not one of Colin's excuses for a trip to The Kings Arms) and so I approached the bank of the stream looking for a way down to the water for a quick drink. All along that stretch, the bank was mostly quite steep but I eventually spotted a route down via a little gully which descended to the stream's edge. There, a couple of flat rocks made a makeshift platform from which I could easily lap up the cooling water. So down I popped, and whilst I initially slipped slightly on the rock as I landed, I quickly regained my balance and started to enjoy a nice cooling drink.

When I'd done, I turned around to climb back up the bank, only to realise that the way up was significantly more problematic than the way down. With my paws not getting a proper grip on the now wet rocks, I leapt up, only to feel my claws scraping into the loose soil as I landed at the top of the gully, and back down I quickly slid. Worse, when I arrived back on the wet and slippery rocks, my trajectory took me sliding helplessly into the stream. Now a raging torrent it most certainly was not, but the flowing cold water came right up to my undercarriage and I struggled frantically to get any purchase on the sand and pebbles beneath my paws as I tried another wild but unsuccessful lunge towards the bank, and then another. And by this time, Clementina, as well as getting seriously wet I was starting to get seriously frightened, so much so that I saw my life flash before my eyes (at least I thought it was my life – it was a very quick flash really, and with very little in it, if truth be told) and a vision of the Rainbow Bridge was just starting to crystallise in my mind when – whoosh! – up I was lifted, out of the water and into the air by Colin's most welcome hands.

As he carried out his dramatic rescue act, the Old Man was precariously poised, one foot on a rock and the other in the stream, as he half-passed, half-threw me onto the bank where a seriously worried-looking Monica welcomed me gratefully into her arms. Loving hugs and cries of delight followed as Colin clambered out, with one soggy boot and a saturated trouser-bottom squelching as he went. "You could have ended up in Morecambe Bay, there, Stanley," he told me sternly, but with obvious relief in his voice – well, I've no idea where Morecambe Bay is, but if, as I suspect, it's another name for Kingdom Come, I was in full agreement with him on that one.

Once we'd all settled down a bit and gotten over the shock, Colin duly delivered, in a rather haughty voice, a short lecture concerning the First Law of Streams and Rivers, which states, quite simply, "Don't jump into them unless you're sure you can get out."

Anyway we all arrived home safe and well, with a couple of treats served up to help me get over my trauma. And let me just say that I'd be the first to admit that, in a perfect world, my gratitude for my salvation at Colin's hands and his saturated foot should have stretched to me ignoring his damp and lonely sock as it lay quietly drying on the radiator in the kitchen, just within my reach – and yes, I fully appreciated that he'd been heroic, and I know that said sock was half of a rather expensive pair of Brasher Fell Masters he'd not long purchased but, as you know, instincts are instincts, and socks are socks, and puppies are puppies. I'm sure I don't have to draw you a picture of how it all ended up, but suffice to say that an early trip round the corner to the hiking department at The Larch Tree is definitely on the cards.

Still, Colin did have his moment in the sun to go with his foot in the cold water. As we toured the pubs of Cartmel that evening, and successive pints of beer were duly despatched, the degree of his heroism that afternoon increased significantly with each telling; so much so that, by the time we got to The Pig and Whistle just before closing time, there was talk of nominating him for an RSPCA award for bravery, above and beyond.

Anyway, we'll be back down in Manchester in a day or so and can catch up.

Yours, as ever,

Stanley

Heaton Road
Withington

12th September

Dear Clementina,

I don't know why the word 'stripping' causes such excitement in this house, but it certainly does. Now as you well know, it's the accepted wisdom that we Borders need to be stripped of our outer coats on a regular basis, so why such a straightforward procedure should be the cause of such levity on Colin's part is anyone's guess.

It all started, you'll recall, when you turned up in the park the other day looking very trim and tidy. Jan explained that she'd decided to try stripping you herself and, with advice she'd found on a website, she'd obviously mastered the art in no time. So when Colin got back to the house, he immediately volunteered to research the subject on the internet and off he popped into the study. Well the best part of an hour had passed before he emerged to announce that, after much sifting and searching, he'd found the site that Jan had recommended. Particularly unimpressed, Monica suggested that next time he should add the words 'Border Terrier' to 'stripping' into his search engine so as not to waste time, but he didn't appear to be listening.

Anyway, she duly studied the site and meticulously followed the online instructions and, for the most part, the whole process went swimmingly well. It transpired that her adopted method was to gently tug at little clumps of my hair whilst I was lying on the sofa in that trance-like state that comes so naturally to us puppies, and after a couple of sessions, my back, shoulders and legs were looking as dapper as a show dog at Crufts.

The problems started, however, when she shifted the centre of operations to my undercarriage and associated regions. As perhaps even you can appreciate, a gentle tug of one's fur in one particular area can be a real delight to the senses, whilst the same effort a few inches further south can be painful in the extreme. And so it turned out to be on this occasion, as we entered the second and less impressive phase of Project Strip Stanley.

Now Jan had told Monica that the whole procedure was 'just like plucking a chicken', and while that may well be technically true, Clementina, you have to appreciate that a chicken in the process of being plucked will have been deceased for some time, unlike a Border puppy such as myself who was merely dozing when the pain struck; and let me assure you, the agony of a 'pluck too far' would have even brought tears to a dead chicken's eyes! It's not often that I emit a loud and painful yelp, but that's exactly what I did on this occasion, which led to the whole exercise being suspended and placed under review. And as you'll see when next we meet up, I now sport a very nifty short-back-and-sides, set off by some long straggly bits in strategic places – though I think you may find the overall style rather fetching, actually.

On a completely different matter, Clementina, have you by chance come across tomato sauce in your travels around your house? I ask because there's a debate going on at the moment around the delicate issue of fox poop and my alleged infatuation with it. As you know, rolling in the deposits of Mr Reynard in the park is something that, in my opinion, is down to the principle of 'a dog's gotta do what a dog's gotta do', and when Colin declares, "Why do dogs do that?!" my immediate thought is, *Why don't you humans do it, more like?*

Now I'm sure I've mentioned before that Colin is a bit of a 'smarty pants' at times, so much so that Monica is only half-joking when she tells her pals that she sold all her encyclopaedias on eBay, having no further need for them as Colin knows everything. That's a bit unfair on the Old Man, in truth, but he does spend a lot of time researching on the internet (albeit that Monica has banned any future 'strip' searches). As a result, he now reckons that my ancestors, the wild wolves of old, still have a big influence on my behaviour, and my wallowing in the essence of the gunge of another creature is an instinctive desire to disguise my scent as if I'm stalking wildebeests as they roam over the African Veldt. Monica has pointed out, however, that being smothered in unmentionable muck may equip me well on the off-chance that I come across a geriatric gnu gently grazing upon the council football pitches in Fog Lane Park, but it effectively vetoes my right to wander freely around the various rooms of Heaton Road.

So to try and deal with the problem, they followed the principle of prevention being the best cure, with Colin sporting a water pistol to squirt at me as soon as I looked as if I was about to wallow about in some unidentifiable mess. He quickly stopped that particular practice, however, not only because he realised that I could happily indulge myself in the undergrowth out of his sight and beyond his range, but also because a couple of concerned mums in the kiddies' playground reported to the community patrol officers that they'd seen a suspicious man coming out of the bushes carrying what looked like a gun. All very embarrassing it was to say the least, but all quickly hushed up, thank goodness.

As for the smell, I must admit that it's not pleasant for either party when, upon our arrival home, Colin is required to lift me up to his nose, give me a thorough sniffing and then, with a grimace on a face that makes him a dead ringer for a gargoyle, carry me speedily out into the garden for a lengthy hose-down and a harsh rub with a rough towel. Unfortunately, even this dramatic and at times chilling remedy is not guaranteed to bring immediate relief to their olfactory systems, and hence my reference to tomato sauce. Seemingly, Wiki-wisdom claims that rubbing this commonly found condiment on the affected canine has been known to solve the problem when water can't; but to date the idea of smothering ketchup on a small dog as if it were actually a hot dog is the nuclear option that remains firmly in the bunker. Dog perfume remains a possibility, however – Colin is, as you would expect, researching it as we speak.

See you soon.

Yours, as ever,

Stanley

Heaton Road
Withington

20th September

Dear Clementina,

Gosh, how nice it was to see you back in the park this morning. I didn't realise how much I'd missed you until I saw you scampering towards me across the wet grass, ears flapping as you ran along and your little legs going at twenty to the dozen. Happy days are here again.

Not much has happened since you left for your holiday, although Colin and I did have our own little adventure when we joined a newly formed dog-walking club. I think I may have mentioned before that now that he's semi-retired, he's got more time on his hands and so last week he was very pleased when his old pal, Sobie, invited him to become a founder member of the Chorlton and District Dog Walking Society, which has recently been incorporated with the stated aim of 'wandering the highways, byways and waterways of South Manchester on the alternate Mondays of each month (Bank Holidays excepted) in the interests of, and promotion of, the social welfare of dogs, their owners and their owners' associates.'

"Stanley will love it," declared Colin enthusiastically when he raised the subject with Monica, and my tail was wagging happily at the mere prospect.

Now I'd imagined that Monica would be all in favour of such an idea but, for some reason, she didn't share our collective enthusiasm. It turns out that the pal who has set up the club has, in her words, 'got previous'. "Sobie hasn't even got a dog," I heard her say, "and it'll be just like the other so-called 'clubs' he's set up: just an excuse for a glorified pub crawl."

"That's unfair," responded Colin, rather defensively I thought, but by then Monica was presenting her evidence. It turns out that when men retire, there's a temptation, albeit a minor one, to spend too much of their time down at 'the local' and upon his retirement, Sobie, who had in the past been known to succumb to the enticing charms of the nearest alehouse, was determined that he and some of his fellow retirees would avoid that particular slippery slope. Accordingly they set up several 'cultural societies' to better pass their time. The first was the Chorlton and District Geographical Society which convenes every other Wednesday and travels around the North West of England by means of

concessionary bus and rail passes, "in the advancement of a greater geographical understanding of the region," by visiting a number of inns and public houses en route. An associated club, the Chorlton and District Historical Society, meets on the alternate Wednesday in order to visit the many older and historical public houses of Greater Manchester, "the better to appreciate the role and historical context of such institutions." Anyway, despite Monica's cynicism, Colin decided to give the motives of his pal the benefit of the doubt and so, on the following Monday, he and I duly turned up on the banks of the Mersey for the inaugural meeting of the CADDWS.

To be honest, I suspected almost immediately that Monica may have had a point after all, based on the fact that, whilst Sobie and four colleagues had turned up all nicely kitted out for a ramble, there was a distinct absence of any other canine involvement – in fact, the sole representatives of the 'dogs and their owner' cohort were me and the Old Man. It turned out that that none of the group actually owned a dog and, whilst this had initially been seen as a problem to establishing a dog-walking group, it was not deemed an insurmountable one; indeed, my recent arrival in Withington had provided the perfect opportunity to fulfil their ambitions.

I have to say that I personally didn't see the absence of other dogs as an issue, especially as I was now the centre of everyone's attention, with them all heartily welcoming me into the pack with effusive strokes and rubs and pats and greetings of, "Hiya Stanley!" and, "Who's a good dog then?" After the initial induction was over, the seven of us happily set off with a jaunty gait along the banks of the Mersey, with each member ceremonially taking it in turn to lead me along the riverbank on the long leash, so as best to fulfil the stated objective of the society.

Sadly, I fear that this first ever meeting of this esteemed organisation will turn out to be its last.

As Monica had so accurately predicted, our lengthy walk involved a significant number of diversions to what were declared to be 'refuelling stations', but which I recognised better as pubs. By the time we arrived home after our perambulations some three hours later, Colin was, to put it mildly, slightly the worse for wear and in fact both of us were suitable for nothing more than flopping down in the lounge and visiting the Land of Nod for a couple of hours before dinner.

"I can't keep this up," he told Monica, resignedly, as he eventually managed to sit up at the table for his evening meal. "Five pubs, we went to!" he continued. "I don't know how they do it. Six blinkin' pints… in three bloomin' hours!"

Monica, as you can well imagine, didn't have to say, "I told you so," as she dished out his food, her bemused expression saying it for her. And so that, as they say, was assuredly that.

When advised the next day of our joint resignation from the society, even Sobie had to admit that a dog-walking club without a single dog was just one concept too far and the enterprise duly folded. I hear that he's now set up the Chorlton and District Musical Society, which will seek to "appreciate fine music of each and every kind, specifically that which is played both live and on jukeboxes in the alehouses of Manchester." Not surprisingly, Colin has declared that his love of his liver is greater than his love of music and he's politely declined an invitation to join the new venture. He has determined, however, to take me for more walks along the Mersey, saying that he seems to remember, albeit rather blurrily, that it was quite nice down there. Maybe you could join us.

Yours as ever,

Stanley

Heaton Road
Withington

29th September

Dear Clementina,

I'm sure you agree that life contains many strange things and I've just discovered another couple – TV and football.

I first came across the TV thing, which my folks sometimes call 'the telly', on my first day here in Manchester. It was sitting up proudly there in the lounge and what I immediately spotted of particular interest were lots of chewable-looking wires and rats' tails coming out of the back of it, and I must say I was rather disappointed to observe that these appeared to have been deliberately blocked off from my reach by a strategically positioned fireguard, bought for that very purpose from the local B&Q.

A day or so later I was intrigued to notice that, despite me not being able to detect the smell of any living thing in or around the telly, I could definitely see small people moving about on it and could actually hear their voices coming from inside it. Stranger still, I noticed that Colin spent a considerable amount of time not only looking at it but holding regular conversations with it – in fact at times he became very heated in these discussions and often ended up red-faced and frustrated, shouting at the screen. It turns out that there are two specific occasions when he becomes especially agitated with it; the first is when, face aflush, he's raging at someone on there who I think he called, "You no-good two-faced lying politician," while the second is when he and his pal are watching what I have now discovered is called 'football'.

I first got a hint of what football is all about shortly after I'd arrived on the scene down here. One night I went into my crate around 10.30 but, unusually, Colin stayed up late in the other room and a few pals joined him. I heard them laughing and joking excitedly and speaking about the World Cup, which I initially assumed to be what they were drinking the copious amounts of beer and wine out of. But as I dozed off I did catch a reference to it being something to do with football and something called the, "Bloomin' useless England team."

Anyway, for a couple of months I heard nothing more of it until last Wednesday evening when his friend Ben came round clutching six cans of beer to watch something called The Match with Colin.

For some reason, as soon as Ben arrived Monica took her leave and hightailed it up to her bedroom and my first instinct was obviously to follow her, with the prospect of stretching out on that nice comfortable bed being an enticing one. But my inquisitive nature got the better of me and I decided to hang around downstairs with the lads and see what was going on. And so as the two of them settled down in their armchairs, Ben with a beer in hand, Colin with a large glass of claret, I nipped up onto the sofa and settled down up against a cushion. The game hadn't actually started at that point and, what with them droning on about midfields and formations and whatever, and with the cushion being especially comfy, I soon nodded off. And I was happily dreaming away, chasing foxes through the woods up in Cartmel, when I was woken with a start as the two chums leaped to their feet shouting, "Goal! Goal!" Well, as you know, I'm always one for joining in all things communal, so up I leapt, and "Goal!" I dutifully barked. Now I think I've mentioned before how puppies that jump up into the air have to land somewhere, and it was surely not my fault that in this instance I landed on the coffee table where Colin's large glass of wine had been only tenuously resting. As if to join in with the general air of excitement, the glass duly leapt into the air, with the not unsurprising result that both it and its dark red contents ended up on the carpet.

I'll tell you what though, Clementina, I was truly astonished at the reaction of Colin. His standard response to seeing wine spilt is to observe that he'd 'rather spill blood', so I was expecting some harsh words from his direction at the very least. But it turned out that he was 'made up' (in his parlance) that his team had scored and was, consequently, all sweetness and light. He even went so far as to give me a pat on the head, declaring, "Never mind, Stanley, these things happen; it's not the first time that old carpet has been baptised with vino, and I'm sure it won't be the last." Such munificence on his part was a most welcome surprise and I suppose it just shows how happy people feel when they've had a few drinks and their team scores.

Anyway, obviously relieved by my good fortune, I was by this stage too excited to resume my slumber and so I lay there staring at the TV trying to work out what this so-called 'beautiful game' was all about. And one thing I did suss out early on is that it's definitely not a sport for us dogs. For a start, it all begins when a man blows a whistle and, instead of running up to him as we would all do, all the players run away from him in various directions. What's all that about, then? And, get this – when one of the players gets hold of the ball, instead of keeping it for as long possible like you and I would sensibly do, he quickly gets rid of it to somebody else – how crazy is that? No, I'm convinced that there's no place in a dog's world for football.

And then there's that other game I saw on the TV, tennis – now that really is daft. A big red-haired guy whacked a tennis ball at another guy and then, instead of grabbing it and running off somewhere and sensibly chewing the life out of it, the other fella grunted, "No thanks, you have it," and hit it back to the big guy, who then repeated the madness by whacking it back again! They were utterly bonkers, the pair of them, and after a couple of minutes such was my frustration at their silly antics that I just couldn't watch anymore.

Mind you, a few days ago I discovered Colin watching another game called rugby, and I'd say that that's a far more sensible sport. In it, the players get hold of the ball and quite rightly won't let go of it, even when the other side jump up and down on them. And then everyone chases each other around the field and they all roll about on the grass, tugging at one another and even, on occasions, actually biting each other. And, perhaps most sensibly, they all spend lots and lots of time with their noses stuck up each other's backsides – what fun! Yep, that's the game for us dogs, Clementina. *Swing Low* from now on, I say.

Yours as ever,

Stanley

Heaton Road
Withington

1ˢᵗ October

Dear Clementina,

Talk about 'unexpected items in bagging area!' What a day! There we were this morning, up at the top of the garden, me undertaking my morning constitutional, Monica on hand with her poop bag ("Collecting for the politicians' welfare fund," as the Old Man now likes to term it), when out of nowhere – zap! – we got mixed up in a battle between a gang of wasps and a bunch of bees, and I started to get seriously stung in the crossfire! Now as I may have told you before, that part of the garden has been left completely uncultivated, with weeds, brambles and nettles and the like growing to their hearts' content ("No Man's Land," Colin calls it; "leaving it as nature intended," or, "Lazy Man's Land, more like," as his beloved perhaps more accurately describes it, knowing how averse he is to manual labour), and there's been a ground-bees' nest there for as long as I remember. Well I don't have to tell you that we terriers are usually very keen to put our snouts into whatever holes we come across on our meanderings, and without so much as a 'by your leave', but from the moment I first came across this particular one, a little flying chap in a striped blazer advised me to, "Buzz off and mind your own, my big hairy friend," and, having caught a whiff suggesting he had a few thousand similarly clad mates down there, I didn't have to be told twice.

Anyway, as I was saying, a real ding-dong was developing as we wandered innocently past the hole's entrance this morning and I was duly stung a few times in the melee – not pleasant, I can tell you. But worse was to follow; Monica, with her collection bag now full, was similarly attacked and ended up being stung on the arm. You can imagine how, by this time, the pair of us had started to well and truly panic and we raced off down the garden path towards the sanctuary of the kitchen, shouting and barking as we went, calling for Colin to come and help. And as we did so, Monica spotted a couple of the blighters settling on her sleeve, obviously preparing to strike. Instinctively, she swiped at the assailants with her opposite hand. But, as fortune would have it, that was the hand that was holding the poop bag, and so whilst she succeeded in whacking the offending marauders, it was, as old Clever Clogs was later to describe it, somewhat of a Pyrrhic victory. Those bags, I don't have to tell you, aren't designed to be weapons of war and so, on contact with the little buzzers, this one duly split and splattered its contents all around the place. I won't upset you with the details any further, but suffice to say, Colin ended up having to set the garden hose on us both before we were deemed clean enough to be re-admitted to the house.

I'm sure you won't be surprised to hear that, after such a tribulation, neither Monica nor I were keen for breakfast, and in fact I felt so lackadaisical that, whilst I could just about stand up, I couldn't really move around much. Colin, who knows about these things, was worried that I was going into some kind of toxic shock, and so it was off to the vets we promptly went.

Five minutes later we were sitting in the surgery's empty waiting room, next to be treated, when a young lady rushed in with a cat in a basket. "I'm awfully sorry," she panted, "I should've been here half an hour ago to drop him off. Is it too late, can he still have his operation?"

"Yes, that'll be fine," said the receptionist, reassuringly. "Name?" she asked.

"Colin," said the young lady.

"Yes?" replied Colin, wondering what she wanted of him.

"What?" said the young lady.

"You called out my name. I'm Colin."

"No," she replied, laughing, "That's the cat's name. My mum always gives them daft names."

Now she was far too pretty for Colin to take offence at this rather flippant remark, so he continued, "Is he in for what I think he's in for?"

"Yes, I'm sure; it's the old 'snip-snip'," she replied, imitating a pair of scissors with her fingers.

"Well I hope they don't get us Colins mixed up," he replied, only half-joking I suspect.

At this point the receptionist broke into the conversation, enquiring, "Has he had any breakfast?"

"Is that relevant?" asked the young lady.

"Oh yes," came the reply, "he can't have the operation if he's had his breakfast."

"I've had my breakfast," interrupted an obviously relieved Old Man, loudly. "Bacon and eggs," he continued, "and toast and marmalade to follow," he added, just to finalise the matter.

So that was a potential crisis over for him, but my already eventful day still had a challenge in store. Now as you know, I don't much like going to the vets. It's not that the people there aren't very nice and all that, but there is that pervading smell of fear there, left behind by many a poor worried dog, and it's a smell that no amount of disinfectant seems to be able to clear. But added to that, I'd been in there just the other day for a puppy MOT and I'd had rather an upsetting experience on that visit. I'll spare you the gory details, but suffice to say it involved an ageing vet who couldn't find his glasses, a thermometer with a spike on it, and a young puppy's rear end.

So I wasn't the calmest of puppies as I was put up on the table with a nice young chap checking

through my fur for stings, and when I saw him turn sharply to his instrument tray and pick up the thermometer with obvious intent, I was not happy, to say the least. I've always considered myself to be the most calm and polite of young dogs, but the sight of that implement of torture got me all of a-fluster and, I'm ashamed to say, I started to snap at the vet as he wielded it. What a mistake that was! With a couple of swift movements, the youthful medic had my snout strapped into a muzzle and my backside introduced to Mr Thermometer for the second time in a week. Fortunately, the young man had a good eye and a steady hand, but I'm now thinking that on any future visits to the surgery, I'll go with a muzzle already fitted, and this time it'll be covering the other end to my snout!

Anyway, happy to report that no long-term damage resulted from my stings, although Monica is apparently having to have regular infusions of gin and tonic this afternoon to get her through the trauma, but I'm sure we'll both be back in the park tomorrow and will catch up with you then.

Yours as ever,

Stanley

Heaton Road
Withington

6th October

Dear Clementina,

The students are back! Have you noticed? I only mention it because Colin's become quite exercised by the arrival of hoards of these young things here in South Manchester. I'm not quite sure who they actually are or where precisely they've arrived from, but seemingly there are thousands of them and I can only assume they've migrated here, just like all those birds in the lake in Fog Lane Park. There are a few important things I've learned about them from Colin, however, one being that they are not like they were in his day – now, having seen some photos around the house of him in his student days, I'm sure the latest cohort are very glad about that fact. Another is that they have some very strange habits, not the least of which is seemingly sleeping in the daytime and only coming out at night, like those bats that Billy told us about. And, just like bats, as they move around the streets in the dark, they have to raise their voices and squeak a lot so that their pals know exactly where they are and don't bump into them. I know all this because Colin was complaining last week about them coming past the house at three o'clock in the morning, talking loudly and singing away. In fact, I heard him planning to get a load of his pals and go around one midday to a student house in Ladybarn where everyone will be in the Land of Nod, and all the old guys will stand outside and bawl out ancient pop songs through megaphones, just beneath the bedroom windows.

"Let's see how they like repeated choruses of *Is This the Way to Amarillo* blasting out at a hundred and twenty decibels when they're trying to sleep," I heard him declare; and having heard how badly he sings, I'm sure the answer would be, "Not a lot."

Monica has repeatedly told him to calm down and assured him that, once lectures start in earnest, the young things will settle down. Personally, I've got to say that I've got a lot of time for them. And one thing I especially like is that they really make a fuss of me whenever I meet up with them on my way to the park. Whenever Colin and I come across a group of them on our walk, he usually loudly declares, "Come on Puppy, let's go to the park," and this invariably makes the girls in the group promptly turn their attention to yours truly, crouching down to stroke me, whilst enquiring of Colin what my name is and how old I am and the like. He rather overdoes the age bit, I think, knocking

a couple of months off the true position, but me being the cute little Border that I am, I invariably impress them with my puppyish good looks. (Monica is now seriously worried that Colin's constant concern about my age will see him getting the hair dye out when my whiskers get grey.)

Apparently loads of students have dogs of their own which they've had to leave at home when they set off for the groves of academe, and I can only assume that seeing me brings back the heartache of their separation. As I understand it, being apart from their canine friends causes them real stress when they first arrive at college, which they try to cope with by drinking copious amounts of alcohol before going off to all kinds of dances and events; at these they seek out somebody to later cuddle up with in bed, as a dog substitute, so to speak. I think I may even have heard this phenomenon referred to as puppy love, but I'm not really sure.

Talking of student days, I'm not sure what Colin studied but he's a right old know-it-all at times. I can't recall if I mentioned it but Monica is very keen on visiting art galleries and the like, and apparently Colin once read a *Beginner's Guide to Art* so he's not averse to joining her on her trips and giving her the benefit of his expertise. Anyway, this week I was pleased to be invited along on one such excursion and the three of us duly set off to Yorkshire Sculpture Park. It's a very interesting place is the YSP, with acres of fields and woods, and lots of various statues and such dotted around the place. After half an hour or so we were striding across a meadow when one particular work caught our attention, with Colin suddenly coming to a sharp halt and gasping, "Oh my goodness, just look at that – it's a Henry Moore." Well, I did more than just look at the rather weird-looking sculpture; I wandered over to it and gave it a good all-over sniff before climbing onto the plinth. And then, without further ado, I cocked my leg up against a strut just where 'the infinite and the finite meet in symbiotic harmony', as Colin was eloquently explaining to his wife. "D'you see?" he spluttered, by now truly animated. "D'you see?! That's the mystery and the wonder of Moore; how he reaches into the innermost depths of nature so that even Stanley wants to communicate and express his empathy with the work through peeing on it. I mean, how magical that he should pee just there, at that very junction, where the yin meets the yang?"

As I looked up at him as he continued to wax lyrical, his eyes almost misting over with the intensity of the moment, I mused to myself, *I don't know about that, mate, but from what I can sniff, over the last day or so four foxes, two badgers and at least three dogs have all deemed this a good spot to do their business, so it's good enough for me!*

Monica humoured him, saying, "Yes dear, I'm sure you're right, but can you pass me a pooch pouch – I think Stanley's about to empathise again, and on a grander scale this time."

At that point, the sight of me doing what comes naturally brought him swiftly down to earth from his trip to the Seventh Astral Plain, but he was still harping on about it in the pub when we got back to Manchester, telling everyone I was a true aesthete, whatever that is.

Anyway, there aren't any sculptures in Fog Lane to get our attention, just a few rusty old goal posts, which are getting rustier with every visit, I've noticed. Apparently a local councillor recently blamed us dogs for the rust, alleging it was all down to our peeing on them. Maybe he's right, though I don't know which one of us is responsible for those rusty old crossbars, six foot up in the air, but let me know if you find out; he'll be well worth a watch.

Yours as ever,

Stanley

14th October

Dear Clementina,

Sorry you couldn't make it to the park today but oh boy, did you miss out on Tetley's amazing story about his second cousin Henry, a Border who lives in Prestbury. Six or seven of us had been gallivanting about and what have you all over the rugby pitch when Tetley called us all down to the wood side where we duly gathered around, all ears and panting tongues, as he told us his tale which involved his cousin, a bark from the depths, and a hole too far.

Now I don't know about you, Clementina, but I'm not a great one for barking. I know it's a dog thing which is very common in some of our pals, Barkley in particular, but I like to think that I am, by nature, a quiet little chap, although it's true that there are a few things which cause me to snap and snarl. For example, there's the awful vacuum cleaner thing that, whenever it appears, repeatedly roars at me as it moves aggressively backwards and forwards across the carpet, so I always respond with like for like. And mops and brushes aren't much better; whilst admittedly they're less noisy than their electric chum, whenever either of them appear they always seem to be challenging me to, "Come and have a go if you think you're hard enough," and so I don't hold back from giving them the 'canine verbals' big time. But other than the vacuum, and the brush and the mop, and maybe the occasional cat or squirrel, or perhaps an unsociable puppy, I tend to reserve my bark for the chime of the front doorbell. Now interestingly, the first few times I barked at said bell I noticed that I didn't get the usual response from Colin to, "Be quiet, Stanley!" which would normally follow a random bark, so I quickly learned that it was an OK kind of thing to do, being perfectly in keeping with our 'guard dog' role. Consequently I now do it on a regular basis and so, getting back to Tetley's tale, fortuitously does Cousin Henry.

Seemingly, he was out with his owner walking off the lead in leafy Cheshire the other day when he came across what he thought initially must be a Doggie Heaven – it was a huge grassy meadow with rolling hillocks and almost a hundred assorted rabbit holes dotted across it. Now, as you can imagine, the gang of us gathered around listening to Tetley were all salivating at the very thought of such a place, and it came as no surprise to hear that Henry had run around the field like a mad thing, scampering from hole to hole, snuffling first down one, and then another, like the good terrier that he is. But Henry's dream site soon became a nightmare when the intrepid little explorer scuttled down one hole too many and, horror of horrors, didn't come back up! And, more frightening still, such was the speed of the little man as he scooted around that his owner couldn't work out which of the myriad of burrows he'd disappeared into!

Well, after what seemed like hours of frantically and fruitlessly racing around and calling out his name down as many holes as possible, the distraught owner eventually ran home and called the Fire Brigade – apparently you call out this esteemed organisation if your cat's stuck up a tree, your dog's stuck down a hole or your small child's got his head stuck in park railings; good to know for future reference. Anyhow, can you believe it, for three long days the fire bobbies prodded long bendy sticks, with little lights and cameras attached, down what must surely have been each and every burrow, turning up no more than dozens of frightened bunnies, fourteen empty plastic water bottles and a dead badger – but neither sight nor a sound of Henry.

Then, just as they were all about to pack up and tread despairingly away, one of the firemen had a brainwave. "Is there anything he barks at?" he asked the owner, whose face suddenly lit up as she cried out, "The front door bell! He always barks at the front door bell!" With that, she rushed home and, I kid you not, dismantled the bell and took it back, batteries and all, to the meadow. Ingeniously using a megaphone to enhance the sound, the rescue team then moved from hole to hole ringing Henry's bell, and, joy of joys, after twenty minutes they heard our by now much weakened hero raise an exhausted bark from deep down in the darkness. And soon after, two strong men with two big shovels sorted things out and, hey presto, like a bedraggled rabbit out of a hat, Henry was pulled out by the tail from what had so nearly ended up as his grave. Well, you can just imagine the jubilant scenes there in the meadow, as owner kissed dog, then owner kissed firemen, then firemen kissed dog, and then the firemen kissed each other. And what a party there was that night at Henry's house, although he, understandably I suppose, retired to his basket early and missed most of it.

As we listened to Tetley conclude his story with such a happy ending, we all agreed that, in future, we would all bark each and every time we hear someone at the door, as a testimony to Henry's deliverance, and as practice in case a similar fate befell any of us. Furthermore, we determined, there and then, to spread the word from park to park and woods to woods so that, from here on in, every dog in every house in every town in every country will greet the sound of a door bell with a bark, and remember Henry down the hole as they do so.

Reflecting on it all now, I do wonder what would have happened if it had been me lost down that dark hole. Our door bell can't be detached, so maybe we'd have seen Colin carting the whole front door around on a wheel barrow, with Monica running alongside pressing the bell repeatedly; or, more likely, he'd have been pushing that damned vacuum cleaner on a mile-long extension lead across the meadow calling out my name, and shouting, "Stanley, what have I told you about the First Law of Holes?"

Anyway, it all turned out well in the end, and Henry's become a national hero, albeit one who now has a slight aversion to holes – not surprising, really.

Hope you can make it to the park tomorrow,

Yours as ever,

Stanley

Heaton Road
Withington

23rd October

Dear Clementina,

Cor, did I make a right old fool of myself yesterday! It all started when Monica took me to the local pets' superstore for our monthly shop for all things canine, and we enjoyed a carefree ten minutes wandering up and down the aisles, testing the occasional squeaky toy and checking out the contents of the treat bins. This is an exercise I especially enjoy because when Monica is scooping treats into a bag, some invariably drop onto the floor and I'm right there and on 'em before you can say, "Squirrel!" So I was certainly one contented dog, happily finishing off a bony-biscuit as we queued in a line to pay for our purchases. But then, just as I was licking around my lips to safely gather in any remaining crumbs, I happened to glance around and, wow, I saw a huge black-and-white tom cat staring at me! And when I say huge, I mean really, really huge – twice or three times as big as your average moggy.

　I don't mind telling you, my friend, that I was seriously shaken at the sight of him and immediately defaulted to barking mode, just to warn him off, you understand. Well I barked and barked, but he moved not one muscle, and just continued to sit there, smirking at me. By this time Monica was getting rather embarrassed by my reaction and tried to shut me up with a, "Be quiet Stanley, it's only a photo!" Now I've no idea what a photo is but I do know that this thing scared 'seven kinds' out of me, so I just kept right on with my verbal protest of snarls and barks. But he didn't back off one little bit, and just when I reckoned that matters couldn't get any worse, they actually did when the other people in the queue started pointing and laughing at me! Now as you well know, Clementina, we dogs would rather be beaten with a big thorny stick than be laughed at, so my temper was getting worse by the second and I kept on with making a racket. Then, in a misguided effort to try and rescue the situation, Monica started pulling me towards the offending creature, still going on about it being 'just a photo' and trying to convince me that it was perfectly harmless. But that was a step too far for me, I'm afraid, and I slumped myself down on the floor and went into strict survival mode. As you know, when in danger, it's fight or flight by my book, but when you can't do either, as in this case, it's squat down and don't move an inch, and utter a pathetic whimper if you think it'll help, so that's exactly what I did. A by now highly embarrassed Monica seemed to get the message at that point because we swiftly turned our back on the offending creature and I was half-led and half-dragged over to a different checkout, well out of sight of the feline monster. There we duly paid and left the store in relative peace, and a regular supply of titbits in the car going back ensured that when I arrived home soon after, I was calm, cool and, well, just a tad bilious, if truth be told.

Now I don't have to remind you that I haven't always been so anti-cat. In fact, I'm sure I mentioned to you that I actually shared a house with one when I was born, up there in Debbie and Mick's place in County Durham. Alongside Mum, two of her brothers and seven of us puppies, there was Max, a rather sad-looking ten-year-old long-haired ginger tom who spent most of the time asleep on top of the sideboard. Mum told me he wore a hangdog expression because he'd lost three of his essential bits whilst still relatively young. The first two were removed in an organised visit to the vets at six months old, but the loss of the third was far more traumatic, and no doubt eye-wateringly painful, occurring when he had to have his bushy tail amputated at the age of two. He'd jammed it between the forks of a branch when falling out of a tree during a dawn raid on a blackbirds' nest, and Mum was convinced that he'd never fully got over the ignominy of having to be rescued from hanging there, nor over the sad loss of such a beloved appendage. I didn't normally have an awful lot to do with Max, though he did make occasional visits to our puppy pen and we exchanged fairly amicable sniffs several times; and I recall that he was always polite and kept his claws in. Indeed I can honestly say that our brief liaisons left me with a general attitude of mild indifference to him and his feline kind which I carried with me down here to Manchester.

However my attitude changed dramatically last week when, accompanying Monica on a visit to a pal's house, I came across Lucky, a one-eyed cat who was dozing contentedly on the sofa in the living room. Now, with no reason to believe that Lucky would be anything but well-mannered and polite like Max, I approached her to introduce myself, like a courteous puppy should, only for her to suddenly leap up with the nastiest of hisses and viciously lash out at me with her extended claws. Fortunately, through a mixture of luck and my speedy reflexes, her ferocious swipe caught nothing more than the fur on my neck and I was able to rapidly retreat to a place of safety just behind Monica's legs before the cat could do any real damage. But whilst physically I was OK, I'm convinced that psychologically I was seriously scarred by the experience, and Monica is certain that my recent fear of 'the photo' was a reaction to Lucky's malicious and unprovoked attack.

I'll tell you what, though – the whole unhappy episode has set me asking the question, what is it that people see in these bloomin' cats? As far as I'm concerned, other than an undeniable cuteness when young, they have few, if any, redeeming features. I mean, just look at their behaviour – there they are one minute, all sweetness and light, lying on the mat in front of the fire, purring away and doing their harmless-kitten-playing-with-a-ball-of-wool impression; and the next, they're off, prowling around the garden, ripping the throats out of innocent baby birds, or disembowelling some harmless little shrew, just for the fun of it.

And talk about fair weather friends! It's all, "Hello Mummy, hello Daddy, what's for tea?" as they swagger into the kitchen and lean lovingly up against their owners' legs. But if it turns out that what's for tea isn't a big pouch of their favourite gourmet delight sprinkled with kitty treats or whatever, they give their bowl the most disdainful of sniffs before turning tail and, without so much as a by your leave, head off next door in search of richer pickings.

And, I ask you – can you seriously imagine a cat ever 'doing a Greyfriars Bobby'? I take it that you've heard the story of Bobby, the Skye terrier up there in Edinburgh who devotedly waited in vain at his master's graveside for fourteen years? Now it's certainly true that he apparently wasn't the brightest dog in the world ("The last puppy in the litter to open his eyes," as my Uncle Paddy would say) but can you imagine a cat displaying such loyalty? Fourteen years? You'd be lucky to get them to hang around for fourteen seconds, and then they'd be off, scrounging around the nearest fishmonger's bins, or rubbing themselves up against the next gullible sucker with that 'butter wouldn't melt in my mouth' look in their big round eyes. No, there's no doubting it in my mind – "Cometh the hour, goeth the cat," is their motto. You can take it from me, Clementina – you can't trust a cat as far as you can swing it.

Anyway, see you tomorrow, weather permitting.

Yours as ever,

Stanley

Cavendish Street
Cartmel

1st November

Dear Clementina,

"Winter draws on," Colin declared yesterday, as Monica tugged up her thermals before we set off for our morning walk.

"Old joke," she said, dismissively.

"Old drawers," came his pithy reply, but winter, it seems, has undoubtedly arrived.

Now as you know, both you and I were born last winter but I for one certainly never ventured into the great outdoors until early spring, so this change of season, with all these shorter days and colder temperatures, is a new experience, but not, I must say, an unpleasant one. I especially like running round with the gang through the layers of fallen leaves in the park. They come up to my ears at times, although I'm not sure that Monica appreciates it when I do my business in six inches of decaying foliage and she has to spend ten minutes tiptoeing around looking for it.

It turns out that we're not the only ones to have fun in the winter. Seemingly, to cheer themselves up on the long dark nights, people organise parties and festivals and we had one just last night. Strangely, unlike most of the do's at Heaton Road, this one didn't find Colin and his chums imbibing lots of alcohol and talking loudly, but rather involved Monica giving chocolate treats to bands of little children from the neighbourhood who came knocking at the door in the early evening.

Now you remember chocolate, don't you Clementina? It's that stuff you snaffled from off the kitchen table which sent you climbing up the curtains a couple of months ago. You'll recall that it kept you awake for most of the night, so I can only assume that they give it to kids to help them run around more and stop them falling asleep so that their parents can spend more time playing with them.

I must admit to a bit of a fascination with children and I've recently discovered a few interesting facts about the little angels. One is that people tend to have them if they can't have a dog for whatever reason, 'dog substitutes' as Colin refers to them. You'll have seen that they're kept very close to their mums and dads when they're very young, but as they get older, they're contained in fenced areas in the parks and school yards, probably so that they don't molest us dogs too much. Any time I've been in their company, they invariably want to pick me up, and this is an undertaking that they're

61

most certainly not skilled at. They're more than a bit awkward and always seem to wrap their arms around my chest so that my front legs are pointing outwards and skywards, but my undercarriage and back legs are left dangling down, unsupported and wiggling about – it's not an elegant sight, I'm sure you'd agree, nor a particularly comfortable one, to be honest. And have you noticed that they have a tendency to stick their little fingers and thumbs in our ears and keep feeling our noses to check that they're wet enough? This wouldn't be so bad except that it seems that children are born with permanently sticky hands which never thoroughly dry out until they are in their early teens. I assume this is for some kind of evolutionary benefit, maybe to ensure they can easily hold hands with each other, which they are often seen to do, squeaking and squealing loudly as they go along. So all things considered, I reckon children may be harmless enough but they're a pretty poor alternative to puppies.

Anyway, the other evening Monica made her preparations for the expected gangs of visitors, stocking up on chocolate treats and sticking a big, horrible hairy spider thing on the front door. (Apparently before they go out begging, the children play a game at home called 'duck apple', which, surprisingly involves no ducks but does include apples, a bowl of water and a process which Colin says that in other parts of the world is a form of torture called waterboarding.) Shortly after dark, the door bell rang for the first time and I duly ran, barking happily to greet our young guests. But you can imagine my horror as the door opened when, instead of the anticipated little band of kiddiewinks who live down the road, there was a gang of the most dodgy-looking weirdoes and witches that you'd see this side of a haunted house?! Now I know what my job as Guardian of the Front Door involves, and it's to make sure that no rogues, villains or politicians darken our door for any longer than it takes for me to see them off. So at the sight of this wild bunch of baddies, into berserker mode I went, snapping and snarling and barking ferociously, as Colin tried to hold me back by the collar. The unwanted and the undead quickly got the message and were straight off screaming and screeching down the path, arms waving frantically as they scurried through the gate as quickly as their little legs would carry them.

With the satisfaction of a job well done and with tail held high, I then trotted back into the lounge and presented myself, a conquering hero, to Monica. However, for some reason that I failed to work out, she wasn't really as appreciative of my defensive heroics as I'd expected, and for the rest of the night I was disappointingly confined to that room, door firmly closed, whilst she and Colin greeted and treated the youngsters who were by now turning up on the front step at regular intervals. From my by now restricted position I didn't actually catch sight of any of these packs, but I could hear them squealing and laughing, so a good time was obviously being had by all.

We're up here in Cartmel for a week or so now, apparently to get away from the fireworks, according to Monica. I'm not quite sure of her logic, though, because I've seen and heard loads of them up here since we arrived and I'm not really bothered by all their banging and flashing anyhow. In fact one night last week, I raced out of the back door and out into the garden to chase down a fox that was hanging around in No Man's Land. Just as I did so, loads of those rocket things started exploding all over the sky, lighting up the night and making a right old noise. But I can tell you, the flashes and bangs to the left and right weren't going to put me off my quest and I just carried on regardless, barking as I went, off down the garden, "charging towards the sound of gunfire," as a proud Colin was later to describe it. Indeed, he got very animated by it all and as I galloped along he called after me, "Go Stanley! Forward the brave Borderers!" Sadly the fox got away over the wall, but I'm proud to report that I came through my baptism of fire with my reputation enhanced and any fear of pyrotechnics well and truly put to rest.

Don't know how long we're up here for, but hope to see you soon.

Yours as ever,

Stanley

Heaton Road
Withington

12th November

Dear Clementina,

Sorry we didn't get to see each other yesterday, but the rain really was awful, wasn't it? Colin says that winter's well on the way and the time may come when the only exercise I get is a quick two laps around the lawn and a snuffle around the bramble patch up along the garden wall. And it's in anticipation of such that he's been messing around with the cat-flap on the back door. Apparently Colin and Monica had a number of cats over the decades before they came to their senses and got me, the last one being Ginger, a bit of a big lump by all accounts. Anyway, the flap they installed for him is certainly big enough for a dog my size and Colin's got a notion that, when the bad weather comes, I'll be popping out of it and off up to No Man's Land for my poops and peeps, leaving the pair of them nice and warm and settled inside the house. So yesterday morning the Old Man, master of DIY that you know him to be, got out his old oiling can and his tool box and set to work on getting the flap functioning again.

That afternoon they both planned to pop out for a couple of hours, but before they left, Monica took a nice chunk of cheese out of the fridge and left it on a side-plate on the French dresser to warm up, but not before doing a quick check on the positioning of the kitchen furniture to make sure that it was safely out of my reach. And then, with a curt, "See you later Stanley, be a good dog," she chucked me the usual pig's ear and off out gallivanting the pair of them went.

The scene that greeted them on their return a couple of hours later was, I must admit, a somewhat distressing one. There, on the kitchen floor, were the remains of the plate, all smashed and forlorn; and as for the cheese, that had disappeared completely. And as I joined them in surveying the scene, looking first down at the shattered crockery and then back up at the pair of them as they looked down at me, I could quite understand why it seemed for the whole world like a straightforward open-and-shut case of 'dog-collar crime'. But it soon became apparent that Colin, who as I've told you before, knows everything, wasn't so sure. After a quick assessment of the scene, he stroked his chin knowingly and observed that the only way I could have carried out the deed was for me to have stood precariously on my rear legs on the back of one of the chairs before launching myself in a potentially suicidal leap head-first and snatching the cheese in my jaws.

"He's a Border Terrier, not a bloomin' stuntman," he declared, and I saw no purpose in disabusing him of his observation. Monica was, as usual, more sceptical, but the Old Man was now in detective mode and was down on the floor carefully scrutinising what appeared to be traces of mud around the cat-flap, which, it turned out, he'd failed to lock before they'd gone out. "Something else could have come in through here," he maintained, "like a fox or that horrible black-and-white cat that's always scrounging round." Monica merely huffed and was having none of it, but as she rummaged around in a drawer, Colin declared firmly, "Now let's not do a Gelert here!"

It turns out that Gelert was a faithful hound from a few centuries past who was owned by a powerful Prince of Gwyneth called Lou Ellen (at least that's what I think Colin said). Such was the Prince's trust in the dog that one day, as he went out hunting and a pre-arranged babysitter having failed to turn up for duty, he left Gelert behind in the lodge to look after his baby boy. Well, as luck would have it, a few hours later a wolf was prowling around the lodge beneath an open window and he heard the infant gurgling away inside. Excited at the prospect of an easy meal he leapt up and scrambled through. Once inside, he made his way over to the child's cot and began to sniff around what he was now sure would be his next dinner. But at that instant the creature looked around only to see Gelert, all snarls and teeth, charging ferociously towards him in defence of the child. Fast forward an hour or so and the Prince returns; entering the nursery, he was greeted by his hound, head bowed sheepishly and wagging his tail, but completely dishevelled and with blood and gore all around his jaws. The by now frantic Prince then looked around and spotted the cot overturned, with its blanket strewn across the floor, all ripped and bloodied, with no sight nor sound of his beloved infant. Well, putting two and two together and making five, the distraught father immediately drew his sword and, with a mighty lunge, slew poor Gelert with a single thrust deep into the heart. And as the hound let forth a final despairing howl, the baby uttered his own piercing cry, safe as he was under the overturned crib. Racing across the room, the Prince then discovered not just his child, safe and well, but also there, half-hidden in a corner, the blood-soaked corpse of the savage wolf, lying with its throat all torn out where it had been killed by the heroic Gelert! "Tragic it was," observed Colin as he concluded the tale. "He never smiled again, that Prince," he continued, wistfully, "so don't you go doing anything drastic that you might live to regret."

Monica, still rummaging around in the dresser, declared disparagingly that he should stop wittering on, saying that she wasn't searching for a sword but, rather, for the superglue. "I think I may be able to fix that cheese plate," she concluded, "as long as Stanley hasn't eaten any of the broken bits." *As if I would*, thought I.

So as it turned out, in the absence of any conclusive evidence it looked like I'd emerge from the whole incident without a stain on my character. But as fate would have it, ten minutes later I was out in the garden playing a quick game of tug with Colin when the lump of Camembert that I'd swallowed in one gulp about half an hour before, and which had been rumbling about unhappily in my tummy ever since, decided to make a reappearance and up and out it duly came.

Now even Colin couldn't miss the chunk of hardly digested French cheese that now lay accusingly in the middle of the lawn. "Cat's out of the bag now, Stanley boy," he observed, "but let's say no more about it, eh?" glancing as he spoke towards the kitchen window to make sure Monica wasn't watching. And, him having swiftly kicked the evidence into the depths of the shrubbery, we then set off back to the house, with him quietly declaring as we went, "As Thomas Jefferson nearly said, my lad, it is better that a hundred guilty dogs go free, than one innocent dog be condemned." Well I don't know who this Thomas Jefferson is, but he sounds like a wise old chap to me – and I bet he likes dogs.

Anyway, no more cheese for me – or for poor old Gelert, I imagine. Never mind.

See you tomorrow, weather permitting.

Yours as ever,

Stanley

Heaton Road
Withington

20th November

Dear Clementina,

Sorry you couldn't make it to the park today, but what a day you picked to miss. When I first got there at ten o'clock there was already a big gang over on the rugby pitch, all surrounding Suzie, the Border Collie cross, who was telling a quite amazing story – it turns out that she'd only gone and killed a squirrel, and in her own back garden too!

Now, personally, I have no more than a passing interest in squirrels. On the few occasions I've chased them they've just scampered up a tree, and, as you'll appreciate, we terriers aren't really built to catch such arboreal critters, nor to even strain our necks looking up after them; no, we're more concerned with things that bolt down holes, rather than scoot up trees. But, as you know, there are lots of the pesky varmints in the park, and greyhounds such as Blue and whippets such as Poppy seem to love chasing them. I've seen both of them come close to catching one on many an occasion, but the critters always escape up the nearest tree with their nuts and the rest of their accoutrements intact, so to hear that Suzie had succeeded where so many had failed was intriguing news indeed.

The story, however, was not quite as you might expect. As I said, the whole episode had taken place in her garden where a good few squirrels hang out and she regularly amuses herself chasing them down the lawn until they invariably escape up into the big cherry tree down at the bottom. But yesterday, as they went through what had become a fairly routine scamper across the grass, the unlucky squirrel started to climb the tree, only to find a big black-and-white tom cat squatting on the lowest branch and glowering down at it. Well, understandably, panic set in and poor Squirrel Nutkin ran straight back down again, saw Suzie waiting at the bottom, turned yet again to go back up and then, zonk – it died of a heart attack! Just keeled over, it did, stone dead, and not a mark on it. Well, as you can imagine, Suzie had seriously mixed feelings about the matter. Whilst the thrill of the chase is always fun, she considered the bushy-tailed little chaps to be more for play than for prey, and she was genuinely upset, especially as, upon her return to the garden this morning, she discovered that all the other squirrels had, understandably, pitched camp and cleared off down the road apiece, as also, she noted, had the black-and-white moggy.

She was obviously unhappy as she explained to the assembled pack that killing a squirrel is a bit like eating your tennis ball; it's something you just don't do because, if you do, you've nothing to chase and fetch tomorrow. But whilst Blue and Poppy seemed to agree with her on that point, having eaten a few tennis balls personally, I wasn't quite so sure.

Anyway, as we were all about to drift off to continue our meanderings, Poppy pointed out how strange it was that Suzie, a dog who had been reared to herd sheep, had ended up killing a squirrel, whilst she and her kind, bred just for that kind of adventure, had failed to see off a single one of them in the park, despite all of their efforts. But then Kurt and Gertie, the pair of sausage dogs from Didsbury, advised us all that they'd never even seen a badger, never mind chased one, or even knew what one looked like, despite being Daschunds, which apparently means 'badger hounds' in German. We then got to thinking that it was certainly true that many a dog no longer has anything to do with what they were originally bred for. I mean, when was the last time that Barkley was on patrol in a Tibetan monastery to warn the monks of marauding sheep rustlers, or Pebbles ran swiftly beside a coach, as all good Dalmatians were reared to do? Try doing that now and see how long you'd last down on the outside lane of the M56, we mused. And then the bulldogs, Stanley and Sidney, chipped in that they'd have as much inclination to bite a bull on the nose, as their forefathers were bred to do, as they would have to bite a pig on the bottom; that is, none at all!

But at this point, old smarty pants Scruffy, the little poodle, piped up that she came from a long line of 'Puddle' dogs and she regularly fulfilled her vocation by wallowing in the puddles dotted around the parks of South Manchester. And whilst we couldn't disagree, we did all wonder why evolution had produced such a fluffy white dog whose apparent purpose was to wallow about in such dirty, muddy water, with the inevitable result. We could only concur, in our innocence, that the Lord moves in mysterious ways.

Then just as we were all about to go our separate ways, Suzie chipped in to correct us – she wasn't a sheepdog, she pointed out; she was in fact a rescue dog. On behalf of us all, Teddy asked what exactly it was that she rescued, but Suzie wasn't sure. *Certainly not squirrels*, I instantly thought to myself, but decided it best to say nothing at that point, what with her being upset enough as it was.

Anyway, catch up with you soon, as the greyhound said to the squirrel.

Yours as ever,

Stanley

Heaton Road
Withington

6th December

Dear Clementina,

Gosh, isn't life just full of coincidences! I was taking Colin and Monica out for a walk yesterday morning and they'd decided they wanted to go to Lyme Park – you know the place, just the other side of Stockport. You and I have discussed before how important it is that our folks get enough exercise, so when they suggested a five-mile romp across a country estate I jumped at the idea. (In fact I jumped a little too high, to tell the truth, and knocked Colin's mug of tea out of his hand, but it only took him one minute to stop cursing and another two to change his soggy trousers, so no real harm done.)

Anyway, off we set and after half an hour in the car we drew up at Disley station car park. Just as we did so, a family in the next bay were getting out of their car and, hey, guess what – they had a Border Terrier too, a youngish pup called Zac. Well, Zac and I duly made our introductions and, as we made our way towards the park through a big gate, we were suddenly confronted with such a sight as you just would not believe – mingling around the entrance, I kid you not, there were loads of Borders, fifteen or sixteen at a guess, all snuffling around and chatting away on the footpath. Now what are the odds on that? A dozen and a half of us, all going for a romp in Lyme Park, all at the same time and all on the same Saturday in November? You couldn't make it up!

Well, as fate seemed to have thrown us all together (and not for the first time, apparently), we quickly agreed that it would be best if we set off together, so as best to keep the people with us safely grouped, especially as some of them looked as if they might struggle if they were to embark on such a strenuous trek on their own. So with leads formally attached, bootlaces tightly fastened and rucksacks firmly secured, off we all set into the wild green yonder, busily introducing both ourselves and our tail-hinges as we went. And after a short while, once we were in the park and away from traffic, it was deemed safe to dispense with the leads and off they duly came, leaving us all free to charge around to our hearts' content, like a pack of wild things.

Up and down the hills and dales we went, over streams and walls and stiles, and it was really great to see all the people grouped as a big gang. They certainly seemed to get on really well together,

69

young and old, with no fighting or arguing and definitely, I'm glad to say, no dry-humping (which is more than can be said for one or two of us dogs, I'm embarrassed to say, but we'll not dwell on that).

Now us being a sizeable pack of Border Terriers on the prowl, our thoughts naturally got around to hunting a fox or two. Watson, a pup from Stoke, was especially keen to chase one down and he spent the first half-hour running off across fields and up hills in what eventually turned out to be a fruitless quest. He eventually slowed down and started snuffling around with the rest of us after Max, a wise old cove who'd 'been around the block', as he liked to describe himself, advised us that all the foxes who used to live in Lyme Park had moved out some time ago and set up homes in the nearby suburbs of Manchester and Stockport. Max explained that he wasn't daft, old Mr Fox, and he'd worked out years ago that it was far better to live in some harmless old lady's back garden in Altrincham than it was to spend your life on a cold and windy hillside, with the constant fear of imminently being chased to death across the countryside by a pack of snarling hounds and a gang of angry people on horseback. And what was easier, he asked, risking getting a backside full of shotgun pellets from an angry farmer as you tried to steal one of his scrawny old chickens, or spending your evenings happily rummaging through the bins of a drive-in takeaway in Chorlton, feasting on the seemingly endless supply of chicken leftovers of the Kentucky Fried variety?

One creature we did come across, though, was a stag or rather, to be more exact, a gang of them. We'd caught their scent as we mounted a hill and got sight of them as we topped it. They were a hundred yards or so away, hanging around in a large patch of bracken, mumbling amongst themselves and looking menacingly in our direction. Now as most of us had never seen such things before, and with them looking a bit like horses with tree branches sticking out of their heads, we all halted in our tracks, unsure as to what to do. But once again, Max was on hand to educate us, and after he'd given us a graphic description of what those branches could do to a small dog's vitals, we all agreed that discretion was the better part of valour and so off we all went in the opposite direction, with ne'er even a bark or a backward look.

We finally ended up back at the cars just over three hours after we'd set out and, after lots of parting sniffs, we all set off for home, tired but happy, and barking our fond farewells as we went. Colin was full of it on the drive home and kept going on about what a great time we'd all had. I've heard Monica say before that for him there is no such person as a stranger – just someone who hasn't heard all his corny jokes yet, and he'd certainly been able to regale a few of his fellow walkers with what he refers to as his 'classics'. No doubt he'll be looking for other opportunities to ramble on, in every sense of the word, just like he did yesterday.

The only downside to the day was that I was a bit sickly when we got home. It turns out that a nice lady on the trip had given Monica a 'vegetable pig's ear' for me to try. The lady's dog, along with thousands of others, loved this rather specialised treat which looked for all the world like the genuine article, but unfortunately it didn't go down very well with me – or more accurately, it went down well enough but then came back up again, all within an hour or so.

"What's he been eating?" asked Colin, as he examined the evidence on the study carpet.

Monica told him, adding that, "It was just like the real thing, and certainly didn't look like vegetables."

"Well it definitely does now," he replied, as he dutifully cleared up the regurgitated remains. Mind you, the whole day seemed to take its toll on the Old Man and he didn't move off the sofa for most of the next day. It took me all my time to get him to play a few games of tug, so it's certainly worth remembering that we'll have to be careful not to overtire them on these long walks.

Yours as ever,

Stanley

Cavendish Street
Cartmel

28th December

Dear Clementina,

Now whilst it's no doubt true that dogs aren't just for Christmas, having just experienced my first one I'm seriously in two minds as to whether or not Christmas is for dogs – dear oh dear, what a right old palaver it's all been up here in Cartmel!

I suppose I can just about put up with having to pose for the obligatory Facebook photo wearing the plastic reindeer antlers (*suitable for puppies and small dogs*) as well as the Christmas doggie-coats that can only be fitted by almost dislocating a canine shoulder or two, and getting presents is certainly good fun, and I definitely have a penchant for turkey and the trimmings, but as for the rest of it, it's nothing but trouble as far as I can see. And, as seems to be ever the case in this household, we had yet another little drama for which, you'll not be surprised to learn, yours truly got the blame.

The whole Yuletide experience started innocuously enough, with Colin taking his elderly mother to the carol service on Christmas Eve. Now he doesn't usually 'do God', in truth, only ever calling upon the Almighty for divine intervention when his football team is involved in a crucial penalty shoot-out; and the fact that his team has invariably lost each and every shoot-out which they've been involved in has, over the seasons, steered him unswervingly into the agnostic camp. But come the festive season, belting out *Oh Come All Ye Faithful* up at the Priory Church, with a candle in his hand and several large Harvey's Bristol Creams in his tum, is guaranteed to bring out his normally well-hidden spiritual side. And after a few large mulled wines in The Priory Hotel before his return home, he went happily up the stairs to bed repeatedly singing the first verse of *Little Donkey*, having first bid me farewell with a pat on the head and a, "Night-night, Stanley, lad – let's see what Santa brings you tomorrow."

As it turned out, it was difficult to see anything at all the next day, never mind what Santa had brought, not just because of the fog that Monica and I encountered on our early morning walk, but also because of the haze of smoke that greeted us upon our return to the cottage. Now we'd spotted from the racecourse that the cottage chimney was belching heavy grey smoke and so we weren't surprised on our arrival back home to find that there was plenty more of it inside, emanating from

Colin's poor effort at lighting a fire. I think I've told you before about his rather underdeveloped manual skills and his inability to set a fire is very much par for the course. Notwithstanding all of his best efforts, in his frustration he often asks how it is that, despite his painstaking setting of lots of carefully rolled-up newspapers beneath really dry kindling wood, topped with suitably sized lumps of coal, all set in a purpose-built fireplace beneath a specifically designed chimney flue, and with several firelighters strategically placed within the whole structure, his attempted fires never seem to light properly and invariably end up as smouldering, smoky messes; whilst in other circumstances, the dying embers of a half-extinguished cigarette end, casually discarded halfway up a virtually barren mountainside, can somehow give rise to a raging inferno that lasts for days and takes the collective effort of the fire brigades of three counties to extinguish?

Anyway, Monica, as usual, soon sorted things out, and once the smoke had been dispersed through the French windows, they all sat themselves down with a mug of tea and a pile of parcels in front of them.

Now this being the first time the pair of them had opened their Christmas presents in my company, I suppose they could be forgiven for taking their eye off the ball, or the loads of wrapping paper casually discarded about the place to be more precise. As you know, Clementina, I'm very partial to a bit of paper in all its forms and am forever thankful to those thoughtful individuals who regularly discard seemingly hundreds of used tissues throughout the parks and woods of Northern England for we dogs' delectation. I have to admit that Christmas paper is not quite as interesting as tissues, but it has a certain attraction and I was well on with my second sheet by the time anybody noticed. Colin's resulting attempts to take it off me were happily doomed to failure as I ran off through the open French windows and was scooting down the garden, still chewing away, before he'd even got properly out of his armchair.

When I returned five minutes later, you can imagine my delight when Monica called me over to the sofa to give me my own presents. Despite my obvious excitement, she wouldn't let me actually open the three parcels myself, but I was permitted to give them a good sniff and half a chew before she unwrapped them and handed them over. The first was a bag of most tasty doggie chocolates, which understandably lasted just as long as it took for her unwrap the second one, which was a vacuum-wrapped marrowbone, stuffed, I kid you not, with *essence of turkey and cranberry sauce*. No sooner had Colin carefully removed the wrapping and handed it over than off I trotted down the garden again, bone in mouth, searching for somewhere to bury it. This caused some consternation for the Old Man as he'd read the label and called after me, "Stanley, bring it back – it's got an eat-by date of March 2015!" Well, you know as well as I do, Clementina, that it's a fact of life that a good

bone, carefully buried, can be resurrected many months, if not years, later, and the idea that this one, which is currently maturing amongst the worms and woodlice under the apple tree, is covered by Health and Safety food regulations is certainly something to ponder.

But it was the third and final present, a small rubber crocodile, orange in colour and squeaky by design, that brought me the greatest pleasure, even though it was later to play a strategic part in our very own 'crisis at Christmas'. Without going into too much detail, after a few minutes of intense and noisy struggle with my new pal Crockie, the sound of kibble tinkling into my bowl caused me to drop him and go toddling off into the kitchen to present myself for a well-earned breakfast. Now, I have to ask you Clemetina, is it my fault that just at that moment Colin's ninety-year-old mum, still recovering from recent heart surgery, stood up with the help of her stick from her armchair and, despite her recent cataract operation which is supposed to have sorted her vision out, failed to spot Crockie who was quietly settled and minding his own business on the floor below her seat? Despite her frail physique, when she put her weight down on my rubber pal he let out what I admit was an alarmingly loud squeak, causing her to fall sharply backwards with a startled scream.

Fearing the worst, Colin immediately ran in from his sprout-peeling duties in the kitchen, shouting, "Stanley! What did you leave that dammed thing there for?" At the same instant I speedily ran back to check that Crockie was unharmed and, as luck would have it, by the time I reached the scene it was apparent that Mum had, fortuitously, fallen backwards into the safety of her armchair, and what Colin had thought were her cries of distress were, in fact, bouts of giggles and laughter. As I snuggled up to her to make my own check, she put her arms round my neck, declaring that she hadn't had such a good laugh in a long time. Colin didn't share her amusement, however (I think he'd had visions of spending Christmas Day in the A&E at Lancaster Hospital) and scowled at me as he commenced to close a few stable doors by picking up the rest of my toys scattered around the floor.

As for the rest of the day, it passed quietly enough. I sat patiently for a good hour beneath the table whilst they had their dinner, the idea of goodwill to all not stretching to me, quite obviously. But once they'd finished, I was treated to my own festive meal of chopped slices of turkey and two chipolatas. It certainly didn't take me an hour to woof it all down and I spent most of the rest of the day laid out in front of the fire. My tummy felt slightly dodgy for a while, though, and I had the distinct feeling that the Christmas paper had wrapped itself around the chipolatas, but a short walk before the sun had set put me right. I then spent a most pleasant evening lying on Monica's lap whilst they all dozed in front of the fire, although how they managed to do so to the sound of thousands of angry Zulus shouting and bawling at them from inside the TV is beyond me.

Anyway, see you soon.

Yours as ever,

Stanley

P.S. Colin got six pairs of socks and two pairs of slippers for Christmas – aren't people kind to think of me like that?

Heaton Road
Withington

5th January

Dear Clementina,

Well, where did that year go? As you can appreciate, there's great excitement here at the moment as the preparations are well underway for a big party to celebrate my first birthday tomorrow. Some party this is going to be, though, with the invitation clearly stating *No dogs, because you'll need to go home in a taxi!* In fact the whole event is gearing up to be focused not so much on a celebration of my birthday but rather on loads of bottles of beer and Prosecco, neither of which I can drink, along with canapés and cake, neither of which I can eat! And as for the cake, made specially by that shop near the vets in Copson Street, well it's tantamount to an insult, if you ask me.

"It says *Happy Birthday, Stanley*, and it's got paws on it," Colin boasted to me after he'd ordered it. But it might just as well read *Happy Birthday Stanley, and keep your paws off it* for all the chance I'll get to have a slice. They know full well that I'm not allowed to eat sponge, or cream, or icing, and so what do they go out and get? Yes, that's right: a sponge cake full of cream with loads of icing on top. You couldn't make it up! It's a bit like all those people who come out of the supermarket at Christmas with a couple of trollies loaded up with cans of beer, and bottles of gin and wine piled high to the top, declaring loudly that they wouldn't bother if it wasn't for the kids! I suppose I'll just spend the whole evening sitting quietly in a corner, with just a pig's ear to keep me quiet as I contemplate my first year on this earth.

In all honesty, I've got to admit that it's certainly been an interesting twelve months, although for my first few weeks I may as well have been blind and deaf for all the memories I've got of that time. What I do recall, though, is that just as I was getting used to having great fun with my six brothers and sisters up there in Washington, and having lots of cuddles from Debbie and Mick who were looking after us all, Colin and Monica suddenly arrived from out of the blue, doing a credible impersonation of Cruella de Vil as they whisked me off down the A1(M) to Manchester. And I do distinctly remember that, as we set off for our trip south, Monica gave Debbie a box of chocolates and Mick a box of tissues, the chocolates because Debbie and her pals like them, and the tissues because big Mick couldn't stop crying as he handed me over. And I think that maybe that's the biggest lesson

I've learned in the past twelve months – when it comes to dogs, men are from Marks and women are from Spencers.

You've surely noticed that when the ladies get involved with looking after us they do so with plenty of love but the minimum of fuss (in fact, I think with their natural talents they'd make very good mothers if they ever put their minds to it). But when the male of the species is called upon to carry out canine custodial duties, boy, do they make a right old song and dance about it. Whenever Monica isn't here and I'm having to look after Colin, it's not easy, I can tell you. What is so hard, I ask you, about measuring out a cup of kibble twice a day? Do you really have to count out every single piece separately? And, excuse me, but is it so difficult to keep an eye on my water bowl to make sure it doesn't run dry? And what *is* the problem with getting ready for a walk that it takes Monica two minutes to do, whilst with Colin it takes fifteen, ten of which are invariably spent looking for my collar or my lead, or, on occasions, both? And then when we eventually arrive at Fog Lane, with him all dressed up like Nanook of the North, he keeps getting mixed up and starts walking anti-clockwise around the park rather than the usual way. Now I know that going that way round is hardly going to cause a tear in the space-time continuum, but it does mean that we end up following you and Barkley at a distance instead of joining up with you halfway round. And I can't remember how many times he's left his pooch pouches in the car, or in his other trousers, meaning he has to borrow one from your lot; and then, when I do my 'recall' trick and run back to him expecting a treat, all I get is a pat on the head and a, "Good boy, Stanley" because he's gone and left the treats in his other trousers as well. What is he like?!

I suppose I'll give them one thing, though – men do appear to be more adept at playing tug than ladies are. Colin's always happy to grab the other end of a squeaky rubber piglet or a piece of knotted rope and spend ten minutes in a good old struggle with me. And I also have to admit that, after the first six months of 'letting me know just who the boss is in this house' he relaxed somewhat and now lets me sit and doze on his lap and, as long as I can control my digestion and not let forth 'an ill wind' as he calls it, I'm OK to stay there for half an hour or so.

Now having thought long and hard about men and dogs, Colin suspects that the relationship may be all to do with separation anxiety, a condition which is certainly prevalent in us canines. As far as I can understand it, being torn apart from a loved one causes deep stress and concern, which can subsequently lead to long-term psychological problems. Apparently there's been all kinds of research done into the matter and the Old Man is fairly sure that this has happened in this case – not to me, mind, but to him. You see it turns out that Colin reckons he was deeply traumatised as a child when, at the tender age of five, his mother took away his beloved teddy bear (which he'd imaginatively named Teddy), a trusted companion who'd been at his side for as long as he could remember and with whom he'd shared all kinds of adventures. Of even more concern was the fact that when he and his beloved pal were split up they didn't even get the chance to say their goodbyes. Colin only discovered his loss one morning when he went to the airing cupboard where Teddy had been drying out after an unfortunate encounter with a window cleaner's water bucket the day before. When the young lad turned up and looked inside, the cupboard was bare and the bear wasn't there! Understandably alarmed, he ran frantically to his mother, only for her to inform him that she'd decided that at five-and-a-half he was now too old to continue in what she considered to be a rather childish relationship with Teddy. She went on to advise him that the bear had, that very morning, been despatched into the care of a much younger child on the other side of town.

And now, having lived silently with his devastating loss for six decades, the Old Man had finally been reunited with his long-lost and much-loved Teddy, reincarnated as yours truly; none other than me, young Stanley. Well, if I'm honest, it all sounds like a load of old tosh to me, but if it helps him cope with life, who am I to disabuse him?

Well that's all for now, my friend. When next we meet I won't be an innocent little puppy anymore – I'll be a mature one-year-old. Yes, I know I'll probably still like playing tug and scampering around like a young 'un, but I think the time has now come for me to act my age. I'm going to be far more grown-up from now on, so no more idle gossip or silly stories – enough of such things.

Anyway, I'll see you and the gang down at Fog Lane tomorrow. Oh, and when we're there, remind me to tell you about Colin and the matching red-spotted bandanas that he's got planned for him and me to wear when we go on holiday to France – Monica is not at all amused, but I'm sure you will be.

See you then.

Yours as ever,

Stanley

"Stanley's letters were written to make people smile, especially my mum.
I hope they've succeeded."